YAHOO

YARNS

by

KIERAN FUREY

© Kieran Furey 1988

Published by
Furey Publications, Curraghroe, Co. Roscommon

ISBN: I 871351 01 4

Printed by the Elo Press Ltd., Dublin 8.

I don't believe that contentment is part of the plot.
. . . the purpose of life must be more than going to
work, coming home and going to bed.

Bob Geldof

Foreword

In spite of its very odd name, this book is intended as a collection of eight serious short stories. Five are set in Latin America, and one each in India, Greece and England. They are simpler and more straightforward than much of what I have written in the past. Most of these stories have a thread of danger and adventure running through them. Other themes surfacing in many of them are love, exploitation and the desperate struggle of people — as groups or individuals — against heavy odds.

Though I still live much of my life in Ireland, I wander a good deal too, and I try to bring back something of life in distant places and among faraway peoples who sometimes think in the ways that we think, and often think in different ways. As technology improves and spreads, more and more windows are opening onto all aspects of the outside world. I hope this book will be one more such window for you.

Kieran Furey,
1988

An Acknowledgement

I have been helped in a lot of ways by a lot of people in many countries and many situations. Generally, the people who helped me were poor, and expected and got nothing in return. Very few of them will ever read this book, though it is they who inspire and make possible this and other books that I write. This seems as good a place as any to acknowledge, at least, that they exist.

Contents

To Fermín

Beginning Again

A little after dawn on the eighteenth, Francisco left home because the word had come that soon the soldiers would come looking for him. He left his little wooden house and his wife María Teresa and his daughters María Luisa and Laura. His one son, Ignacio, who was nineteen and the eldest had gone already six days ago, for he was a leader of the Party Youth in the town and would surely die if they found him.

It was a week since the coup. The number of killings in San Pedro del Monte was already great, though certainly far less than what was happening in the capital and in the coastal cities. The radio and the television did not speak of the killings, but of the patriotic duties of the people, and the Red Menace, and the need for co-operation with the forces of order. There was much patriotic music, and many speeches by the generals, who spoke always of democracy and the restoration of liberty.

Even to speak of the killings on the telephone was dangerous, but Francisco knew about them anyway, for in the morning when he went to the factory there were bodies in the streets with the faces blown away or the intestines spilling out for the street dogs to feed on. And at work the other Party men told him of the things that were happening in their *barrios*. Of the sound of lorries at night in the dark deserted streets; of the green jeeps that roared along the rutted earth roads of the town, full of helmeted troops enforcing the curfew; of the disappearance of heads of families, students, singers and poets of the people; of the case of Manuel Martínez, shot once through each eye before his wife of three weeks in their living-room in broad daylight.

Francisco closed the door gently, so as not to wake his wife or their daughters. He looked for the last time at the paint peeling from the weathered planks of his home, then turned and walked even-paced up the *calle de la Constitución*, as he did each morning when he went to work. This morning for the first time since the coup he met no patrol. Even if he had, the aspect he presented would have been enough to satisfy the soldiers, for he went in his working clothes and his *poncho* against the morning cold and with his plastic lunch-box under his arm.

And if the soldiers went to his house to question María Teresa, nothing unusual could be learned by them, for not even Francisco's wife of twenty years knew of his plan, and would awake to believe him gone only to the textile factory where for fourteen years he had worked as well and as hard as any man in San Pedro.

She knew the dangers, of course, as his daughters did. Well enough to have agreed at once with his instructions, which called for the three women to go by bus that very evening far away to the small coastal fishing village of San Blas, to the house of María Teresa's uncle Carlos. Carlos was a retired captain of the merchant marine, and had contacts in the navy. Not at the very highest level. But high enough for the *golpistas* to leave him alone. Francisco's family would be safe there. They expected him to join them as soon as he had sold the house and arranged for the transportation of the most important pieces of furniture.

This plan had been made on the 12th, before Ignacio left them. But even then, Francisco had not believed that he would join his wife and daughters in the big house of Carlos Gutiérrez, for he knew that only one of two things could happen now. Either the generals would rule by extermination of all opposition, or they would relax somewhat after the initial terror. If they decided to hunt down all the Party people, then it would never be safe for him to remain in the country and, like hundreds of thousands of others, he would have to fly while it was still possible. And if they relaxed even a little in the power and arrogance and completeness of their victory, Francisco would remain to fight the *Junta*, just as the Party would fight them in the towns and the industrial cities of the coast and in the wretched little *pueblos* of the interior and even in the high mountains.

From the *plaza* he took the 7.15 bus to the village of Las Minas. The bus went, as always, overloaded with women and children and hens and the bales and bags and battered suitcases of the people's possessions. After an hour had passed and the settlements had grown sparser and the road narrower and steeper and more winding, the old bus had shed enough of its load so that he could sit with a seat to himself.

It seemed that the greenness grew with the journey, reminding him of a childhood spent in the foothills, though further north. As far as the appearance of these tranquil, winding valleys went, the coup might never have happened. At eleven when he climbed down from the bus in the single dusty street of Las Minas, it appeared to him that indeed the coup had not yet reached the village. There were no soldiers yet, for the

10

killings and the mass imprisonments and the interrogations and the curfew in the cities and in the bigger towns still occupied the time and attention of the army. In time they would come to the mountains.

Francisco would not wait for them to come. In Las Minas he knew nobody, and therefore trusted none. He began at once to walk, for true safety, if it existed at all, could be found only in the high mountains. Francisco was not a coward, but he needed time to think, and he needed to stay free that he might integrate himself with whatever opposition still remained at large.

All day he walked. He walked slowly and deliberately, always upwards and always wearing the woollen *poncho*, for it was cooler at these altitudes. He ate the four sandwiches of cheese and ham and drank most of the bottle of water before the sun went down. Here in the mountains, a man would not die of thirst, whatever problems hunger might bring him.

Certainly he would not be able to buy food, for his money remained with his wife for the journey to San Blas. Fishing in his trouser pockets his hands came out with a few coins. He added the values and found that they came to twenty-four pesos. He laughed out loud and flung them into the trees. There were no shops in the mountains.

During all the hours of his walking, he met only a solitary indian riding a mule, and passed no more than three small timber houses by the side of the trail. With the gathering darkness came a loneliness that whispered to him like the mountain breezes. It whispered to him the things that he knew already in his heart: he was alone; his family was alone; and for the moment at least, his country was alone.

The stars came out and he walked on in the high stony places where no longer any tree grew. He was following a star that had emerged lower than all the others, some way above him in the dark mountainscape. The closer he got to the light, the more cautiously he went, so that not even the sound of his boots on the gravel could be heard. He would welcome the shelter this house could give him, but yet he must go with great care, for it might contain soldiers.

"*Alto!*" He heard the shouted command at the same time the crunch of boots on gravel came to his ears. The voice, he knew, came from the trail somewhere behind him, but he did not wait. Even as the word echoed back from the rocks above, he was sprawled in the sparse scrub beside the track.

They came up, with the sound of many footsteps. When they reached that part of the trail beside where he lay, they stopped. Still

11

lying prone, he could distinguish, dimly, the shadowy shapes of several men on foot. He asked who they were. In answer, they asked who he was.

Rising to face them, he told them in a calm voice that he lived in the house where the light was. One of the men laughed loud and said that was impossible, for he lived there himself. Just then Francisco could see that the men wore *ponchos* and his heart lifted, for this meant that they were not soldiers.

It turned out that one among them was José Luis Castellano, a Party man from San Pedro del Monte, and well known to Francisco. Like three of the other four men in the group, José Luis was on the run.

The house belonged to the *compañero* called Joaquin. It was a big house of stone, and well stocked with wine from the valleys further down. Together the six men went to the house. They began at once to drink. They drank all night, in front of a glorious fire of wood. They drank themselves into a stupor, and soon after dawn broke over the mountains they went to sleep on the stone floor, wrapped in their woollen *ponchos* and warmed by wine and companionship. Waking up one by one in the evening, they set about cooking. They ate all they could, and made great and heroic plans for their little guerrilla group of six that as yet had not a weapon between them, save alone the fowling piece of José Luis Castellano.

In all the four long months of the southern summer that Francisco remained living in that house, not once did the soldiers ever come there. As the weeks passed, equipment reached them from the Party in San Pedro. The small band came in time to possess a pair of light machine-guns, some World War Two carbines, and a little dynamite.

The brother of José Luis Castellano left them to go on a mission to the capital, and never returned, but his wife Anna came up, riding a mule, to join them. There was also a poet, still without beard, who made poems about the things they did. He never wrote anything down, but memorised everything, and had the woman sing some of the better ones while they sat round the fire at night. They worried much about this revolutionary poet, who went by the name of Felipe. He did not know how to handle his gun — an old bolt-action rifle which, they felt, in his hands presented quite as much danger to the *guerrilla* as to the adversary.

Of course, the soldiers had no idea how many they were. They knew only that there was a lingering resistance here in the mountains, and they preferred not to attempt any close contact. Instead they moved some heavy artillery into the village of Las Minas, where they also built a make-shift wooden barracks.

José Luis or Joaquin went down sometimes to buy food and gather intelligence, and with every trip confirmed what the foreign radio stations were saying. There were isolated guerrilla groups in the mountains, but these were not able to knit together into any kind of united or lasting armed struggle. The repression was too intense and too prolonged. Contacts were too difficult to make, and too dangerous. The Party leaders were in hiding, or dead, or in prison, or scattered all over Latin America and Eastern and Western Europe.

From time to time the forces of democracy and liberty bombarded the mountains in desultory fashion with artillery and sometimes even an aircraft or two, but no harm came of it.

The *guerrilla* that now was led by Francisco engaged the soldiers a handful of times. A lot of noise was made by both sides, without ever a casualty being inflicted. Once, in the manner advised by a manual that Guevara had written and that had long since become a classic in Latin America, the six posted themselves individually in different places and rained a thin, sporadic fire upon a small patrol of soldiers from all the different directions. The patrol went to ground to wait out the assault. When darkness fell, the *guerrilla* withdrew to set up an ambush at a point where steep rock overlooked the trail. But the troops returned to Las Minas by another route.

Military resistance had by then virtually disappeared everywhere in the country. It was clear that the generals would remain for some time. The little group decided to disband. Only José Luis and the wife of his brother remained in the country. Two of the others made their way over the mountains to Argentina. The poet went to the French Embassy in the capital. The Embassy got him a flight to Paris, and from there he made his way to Budapest.

Francisco had been using a Spanish priest based in Las Minas as a way of getting messages to his family in San Blas. Now the same priest — a Padre Jorge Castañeda — arranged to get him into a house in the capital being used to shelter homeless foreigners. There he was joined by María Teresa, María Luisa, and Laura.

Though the generals learned where he was, the Church was powerful, and so Francisco left with his family for Madrid. It was there, at the airport of Barajas, that he embraced his only son Ignacio. It was March 11th, 1974 — six months to the day since the generals had unleashed the terror.

13

Francisco settled down to a job and a small apartment, in so far as a man could settle down who was exiled from his country. The wheel had not come full circle. But it was turning. Ignacio was already engaged to the daughter of a trade unionist murdered in the aftermath of the coup. Francisco had a feeling that he might yet see his grandchildren grow in Chile.

The Whore and The Hermit

Soros Koprou was like a thousand other villages scattered around the island. It lay in a long, narrow valley between steep hills clothed in olive trees. The houses were of stone, the roofs of red tile. There was a small olive oil factory, a church, an elementary school, a few old-fashioned food and drapery shops. There was a workshop making rudimentary furniture and a barber's shop for men.

In the way of entertainment there was the *cafenion* of Dimitrios, where the village farmers went to while away the hours in conversation and in sipping *raki* and Turkish coffee. There was the *taverna* of Iorgo, where the men of the village went at night to play cards and drink one or two bottles of *ouzo* or beer. And there was the house of Luli, where the married men went who were tired of their wives and where the young men went with drink in them in the years before they, too, were married.

Near their summits the hills around Soros Koprou became almost vertical, so that not even olive trees grew and the soil gleamed white and naked in the sun. The white soil was pockmarked with caves, and in one of these lived the holy hermit Mikhalis, known to the villagers as Mikhalis, the Mad Monk.

The children and young people of the village had never known a time when the hermit had not been in his cave, alone with God between the olive groves and the sky. Neither had they known a time when the whore had not lived in the little white house that stood alone at the end of the long, dusty, winding street that was the only street in Soros Koprou.

Only the mature and the old remembered a time when the cave of Mikhalis was empty and the house of Luli belonged to her father the priest. Thirty years earlier, the two had been children together. The houses of their parents were within shouting distance one of the other. Mikhalis and Luli had gone to school together. In the evenings they had played in the dusty street together, or helped each other with homework.

15

Luli's father had died early, and so in the village it was the custom that the people helped her mother, the widow of Spanakis, with the harvest work. Every autumn and winter Mikhalis and his father passed many evenings in the vineyards and the olive groves and the orange groves of Spanakis. Luli was often there with her mother.

They finished school on the same day. In those days few people left Soros Koprou, and Mikhalis and Luli were not among those who left to go to the city or to take the emigrant ship. As was customary in the village, she remained at home to help her mother with the housework and the hens and goats. He, too, remained in the house of his father, Spiros Panayotis, to do early the work of a man.

He learned to carry sacks of olives heavier than himself and to deputise for his ageing father at the markets in the town when it came time to sell the barrels of olive oil or the boxes of oranges. He learned to talk with the men in the *cafenion* in the times when no work had to be done, and at night to drink and play cards with them in the *taverna*. He did not see Luli often, because in the village it was not customary for young men and young women to be seen together.

During harvest time in the fields of Spanakis they were careful to work apart from each other. When they met in the street they said only polite hellos. Their feelings for one another were known only to themselves, for the eyes of the villagers, however much they looked, could see only the surfaces of people, and not the feelings within.

There came a winter when the mother of Luli Spanakis followed her husband to his resting place in the neat little graveyard opposite the church. It was a winter with the weather of spring, and hardly a day was lost to the cold rain that came from the north. Already by the end of January, the olive crop of Mikhalis had been harvested and turned into olive oil in the little village factory that belonged to his uncle, and sold to traders in the town.

The father of Mikhalis owned few orange trees, but Luli Spanakis had many, and so in February Mikhalis spent many days in the fields of Spanakis. Luli worked beside him, and the shyness that had grown up between them in the years since they left school melted much faster than the snow that shone whitely on the mountains east of the village.

It was usual for a man helping his neighbour with the harvest to eat in the house of that neighbour, and in this way Mikhalis went with Luli in the evenings to eat in her house. He would go home while it was still light, as the dying sun lit the snow on the White Mountains and turned it a fiery reddish gold. No scandal would therefore arise in the village.

16

They clipped the oranges from the trees with *secateurs* of the kind used at the end of summer to cut the bunches of grapes from the vine. They picked into the same pail and when it was full he emptied it into a big wickerwork basket. When the basket was full he carried it on his back to the house of Luli and tipped out the oranges on the floor of the cellar. After some days the pile of oranges in the cellar grew very large. The wooden boxes came from the town and he began to stay late in the evenings to help her pack the fruit; the big yellow and greeny-yellow oranges in some boxes and the small yellow ones in others. It was because of this that the scandal arose in the village.

Before her death, the mother of Luli had made an arrangement with a wealthy farmer from the next village that one day her daughter would be given to him in marriage. On one of his visits to Soros Koprou it came to the notice of this man, through village gossip, that Mikhalis stayed late in the house of Luli Spanakis. The young priest who had replaced the father of Luli when the old man died, and who was brother-in-law to the rich farmer, was forced to speak with Luli and with the father of Mikhalis.

Afterwards, Luli and Mikhalis could no longer meet. But she did not want to be the wife of the well-to-do farmer, a man old enough to be her father. She sold most of the land, her dowry. She sold also her poultry and her goats. The man's attentions persisted. In desperation to be rid of him, she took from the town first one lover, then another.

This was not the Luli that Mikhalis had known. When he could no longer bear to live in the village that had destroyed her, and when the pain of his own conscience began to tell him that all was his fault because of his cowardice in the face of the village, he left his brothers to run the farm and went away to become a monk.

The order he joined was contemplative and known for producing hermits, some of whom lived in caves on the Holy Mountain. But when Mikhalis left the monastery on the Mountain, he chose a cave, not on the Holy Mountain, but overlooking his own village, Soros Koprou. In this way the village would be always in his mind and he would spend his life atoning for his own sins and for the sins of the village.

He prayed often for himself and for his village, and lived in the extreme poverty demanded by his order and his conscience. His bed was a threadbare blanket. No furniture adorned his cave. In the evenings his youngest brother, Christophis, came with a little food and water and the gossip of the village. The others would have nothing to do with him. They shut him out of their minds and out of their lives.

17

Mikhalis never went to the village. At twilight when the sun slipped below the summit of the hills on the opposite side of the narrow valley and the heat of the day grew bearable, he would emerge from his cave and sit on the ledge outside and look at the red roofs and white walls of Soros Koprou. His mind was full of a great curse for this village and the people in it, but he struggled always to transform the curse into a prayer.

Down below in the bottom of the valley the people of the village waged their own struggle to transform the curse of poverty into the prayer of bread and wine and fish and olives on the table. Luli Spanakis received the men of the village, and from time to time a stranger, or a traveller from another village passing through.

In October the sun still blasted the valley from a cloudless turquoise sky. The first winter rains were still weeks away, and the parched earth lay bare and white as a skull. Sometimes in the evenings a breeze sprang up and blew clouds of suffocating white dust along the street of Soros Koprou. The grape harvest was finished and that of the olives had not yet begun. The older farmers sat in the *cafenion* and speculated about the olive harvest and wondered when the rains would come, as they and their fathers and grandfathers had done for uncounted years, knowing all the while that the rains would come in November as they always did and that their crops would yield about the same as every other year. Iorgo opened the *taverna* in the mornings, and from an early hour the young men would begin to gather there.

One evening in the middle of October, five men were sitting at the round table in a corner of the *taverna*. They had been there all day, drinking *raki* and eating peanuts and engaging in banter and boisterous talk.

Iorgo, the owner, was one of them. He was a huge, gregarious, balding elephant of a man with grotesquely bloated belly, fat hands, and meat that hung in folds from his red jowls and neck. Though he looked much older, he was forty-two and had a son older than the three young men of the village whose company he loved and who now sat in his *taverna*. This son, Grigoris, sat opposite him. Fat like his father, but small, fresh-faced and boyish-looking, he was wearing the olive green shirt and trousers and the high, polished black boots of the army. It was his first leave since beginning his two years military service, and he paid for most of the drinks, which he served himself.

Antonis was his best friend in the village. A student in the city, he had the reputation of having great intelligence and was held a little in awe by the villagers, but he combatted this by spending long hours in the taverna and drinking at least as much as anyone else. He was thin and greasy-looking, with round-rimmed spectacles and long, mouse-coloured hair.

Manolis and Costantis were twins, and made up the remainder of the group. They were small and dark-complexioned and wore their hair cropped short, army-style. Sly and tough, neither had ever been known to let an insult go unpunished, or a drink go unfinished.

The conversation turned to military life and what a man did without a woman in the army.

"Turns a lot of men queer, the army," Costantis said. "Isn't that right, Grigoris?"

"Not right, no," Grigoris answered. "Only them that's bent already."

"And the others, what do they do when the feeling comes on them?" Manolis asked.

"Masturbate," said Antonis. "What else can they do, eh Grigoris?"

Grigoris Laughed and emptied his glass. "There are plenty of things a man can do. There's no scarcity of women in the town."

"You mean whores?" Manolis asked.

"He means whores," said Antonis.

"I mean ladies of the night — girls experienced in the arts of love. You wouldn't understand, Antonis. You have nothing like them here in Soros Koprou."

"Haven't you heard of Luli, Old Boy?" Antonis asked mockingly.

"Anyway, I mostly don't live in Soros."

"Now there's a woman with real experience; could teach any city pro how it's done, and cheaper too," Iorgo said.

"I bet she taught you a few things," Manolis said.

"I swear before God I never darkened her door," Iorgo said soberly. Then he threw his great head back and roared with laughter, his jowls shaking like red jelly.

"And what about you, Grigoris?" Costantis asked. "Do you know the colour of Luli's sheets?"

Grigoris reddened. "There's no man in Soros Koprou that doesn't know the colour of the sheets of Luli Spanakis," he said.

"I suppose there isn't a man in the village that hasn't been with her," Antonis said, searching his mind for any possible exceptions. "Except the priest, that is," he added.

Iorgo wiped the laughter tears from his eyes. "There is one."

"I don't believe you," Grigoris said.

19

"Is he here?" Costantis asked, to general laughter.

"There is one," Iorgo repeated. He leaned forward and rested his elbows on the table. He looked them each in the eye. He sat back in his chair. "Mikhalis," he said. "Mikhalis, the Mad Monk."

There was an explosion of mirth.

"He's right, by God; Iorgo is right," Manolis said.

"Give that man a drink," Antonis instructed Grigoris, pointing to Iorgo.

"I never thought of that before," Grigoris said, getting up to fetch the round of *rakis*. "It's strange, finding out there's someone she hasn't had. It's almost like discovering she's a virgin."

"I'll tell you what it is; it's a damn shame," Antonis said, eyeing them all. "It's a blot on her record."

"We should really do something about it," Manolis said, joking.

"By God, we will do something about it," Iorgo declared.

Grigoris set the tray with five *rakis* on the table. Iorgo seized his between thumb and forefinger. "Here's to Mikhalis and Luli," he said, moving the glass to his lips.

Antonis stopped him. "Wait," he said. Unsteadily, he stood up, taking his glass. "Gentlemen, a toast. To the forthcoming marriage of Mikhalis, the Mad Monk and Luli, the luscious lay."

They stood and, swaying on their feet, clinked glasses. They tossed the *rakis* back and set their glasses down. Manolis thumped Antonis on the back. "Well, hell, let's do it," he exhorted.

They went outside and waited while Iorgo locked up. "To the cave!" Costantis shouted, and he began to lead the way.

"Wait," Antonis called after him. "He'll never leave the cave. Why don't we bring her up?" They gathered in the centre of the street, undecided for a moment.

"No, she won't leave the house with us," Iorgo said at last. "She only does it at home. We would never be able to coax her up there."

"He's right, " Manolis said. "Who ever heard of doing it in a cave?"

"Uncomfortable, I admit," conceded Antonis. "But how do we get him down?"

"That's the easiest part," Iorgo asserted. "We'll just tell him little brother Christophis is sick with the fever and begging to see him."

"Not him," Antonis said. "Little brother Christophis is likely to have visited him just now in the best of health. We'd better say his old mother."

20

"His mother, then," Iorgo agreed.

"Taken bad suddenly, she was, just this very minute," Manolis added.

"But we'd still have to get him to the house of Luli," Costantis said.

"Why don't we tell him Luli is sick and wants to see him?"

"Dying," Manolis added.

"Wants to make a last confession," added Iorgo.

"But wouldn't the priest do that?" asked Grigoris.

"He's away; gone to the city; won't be back for days," Antonis said.

"Luli has only hours to live. Only Mikhalis the Mad Monk can save her from hell everlasting."

"Amen," Grigoris said solemnly.

"Who'll go?" Costantis asked.

"You go," Antonis said to Grigoris.

"I'll go," Grigoris agreed.

The others returned to the *taverna* for a bottle of *raki* with which to make the Mad Monk drunk. Once inside, they decided to stay for a drink.

It was almost dark when Grigoris reached the cave. Half sobered by the climb, he stood panting and sweating at the entrance. He smelled the damp, musty smell of the cave. "Mikhalis," he said. "Brother Mikhalis, come quickly; you are needed in the village."

In the *taverna*, the lamps were lit. Iorgo was behind the bar, his arms resting on the counter. At the round table in the corner sat Manolis and Costantis, arms around each other, singing. At a table in the corner opposite sat Antonis, arguing politics with two young men who had just come in. On the hillside above the *taverna*, Grigoris stumbled among the olive trees. He was careful to stay in front of Mikhalis. He did not want to let him smell the alcohol on his breath, and he could not endure the sour smell from the filthy rags and unwashed body of the monk.

Luli Spanakis was alone, as was now more and more the case with her. When she answered the door, a strange, gaunt, filthy beggar was standing there with the son of Iorgo Karamanlis. When he came into the lamplight she saw that his face was the face of Mikhalis.

Mikhalis did not know the greying, plumpish little woman who had come to the door. Then in the light of the kitchen lamp he looked closely into the lined, worn face and his gaze met the sad, dark eyes of Luli Spanakis. A great lump rose in his throat and a dryness came into his mouth, and his eyes stung. Abruptly he turned and walked away, but at the kitchen door Grigoris blocked him. "Stay, monk," he said. "Tonight you will learn what a woman is. Luli is to teach you. In a little

21

while my friends will come, to see that you have learned well the lesson."

Mikhalis was about to take him by the throat, but then he heard the voice of Luli.

"Would you like to wash before you go, Mikhalis?" she asked. It was the old voice, the voice of more than twenty years before, remembered as the voice of only yesterday. Even the words were the same. Those words she had spoken to him in the evenings after they had picked oranges together.

"I will wash," he said. Trembling, a cold sweat on his forehead, he waited in the darkness of the bare outer room while Luli heated a great pot of water over a wood fire in the kitchen. Grigoris stood just inside the front door with his back to it, watching the well-rounded contours of the woman in the other room. A terrible, strained tension was in the air, palpable as the wood smoke that filled the house. Grigoris wanted to leave, but the thought of the others kept him there. What would Antonis say if he let the monk go back to his cave and spoiled their fun? And what would the twins think of him? Probably they would tell the whole village that Grigoris, the soldier son of the fearless Iorgo, was the only man in Soros Koprou afraid to spend time in the house of Luli.

When the pot was steaming she took it outside and set it down in the courtyard. Mikhalis followed her and began to splash water on his face and beard, but she went back in and returned with soap and a towel. "You must wash all over," she told him. "No one will see you." When he was naked in the pot she came out with a bundle in her arms. "I have clothes for you," she said, and threw them on the ground beside the pot. Then she gathered up his rags and took them inside to burn.

Seizing his chance, Grigoris ran to the *taverna*. But his father was busy behind the counter, and Antonis had gone. Manolis and Costantis were hopelessly drunk. Grigoris's head throbbed and he was glad to leave the *taverna* and go to bed.

Mikhalis stepped out of the pot and wiped his smarting, reddened flesh dry. He put on the loose-fitting men's clothes and went to the door to reclaim his sandals before leaving. But she brought him in and sat him at the kitchen table in front of a steaming plate of potatoes and rice and tomatoes and delicate-tasting octopus meat that looked like chicken.

"You must eat," she said, "for you have not the strength to go back up to your cave."

His stomach accepted less than half the food, but when he pushed the plate away and got up to go he found that she had other plans. "You are not well," she said without looking at him. "You must rest here a day or two until you are better. I have made a bed for you in the outer room."

He wanted to leave. He did not belong in the village. All he knew now was the solitude of his cave. Like a wild beast, he lived alone with nature and belonged to God, not to men. His place was no longer among men. But his stomach was full and his body was clean and covered by fresh clothes, and he could not be angry with her.

"I must leave," he said feebly. "I must be alone with God. I have given my life to Him, and I must be alone with Him so that I can pray."

"You look like death," she said. "You will die in months. Is it not better to live, that you may devote your life to the service of God, than to die for Him? The dead are of no use to God. Stay awhile that I may nurse you back to health, and then you may go to your cave and your God."

"I will stay this night," Mikhalis said.

In the morning she brought his breakfast. "You must stay a little longer, Mikhalis," she said. "There is much to do here. There is wood to be chopped, and trees to water until the rains come. Soon there will be the work of the olives, and then the oranges. There is need of a man here."

Mikhalis remained. At night he slept in the bare outer room with its whitewashed walls and its cool stone floor, and to him it seemed a paradise. In the daytime he worked in the fields and made small improvements to the house. He prayed only in the morning and at night, but it seemed to him that his whole life had become a joyful prayer. His weight increased. He trimmed his beard and the sun and wind brought colour to his face.

Luli kept the house clean and cooked the meals. Whenever a man came to her door expecting to be made welcome in the old way, she turned him away. She looked forward to November; with Mikhalis she would spread the nets under the olive trees and together they would beat the branches with rods until all the green and purple berries lay in the nets; then they would pick out the leaves and broken twigs and scoop the olives into jute sacks ready for taking to the factory. Then would come Christmas, and after that the time of the oranges.

Mikhalis went neither to the *taverna* nor the *cafenion*, and rarely met the people of the village. Whenever he met them, they spoke civilly about the weather or the crops or the health of others in the village.

23

Christophis came often to the house of Luli to see his brother, but the rest of the family would have nothing to do with him.

A great scandal arose in the village. The unsatisfied husbands and the unmarried young men grumbled because now if they wanted a woman they had to do without or go to the town. The men of Soros Koprou were proud of their manhood, and to have been upstaged by a monk was for them a thing altogether incredible.

"Let the Mad Monk return to his cave," they said darkly. "Let him go back to his prayer and fasting. He has no business among us, living a life of ease and comfort in our village."

The spinsters of the village were in shock. When they met in the street, or outside the church on the Holy Day, or at the graveyard where they went to pray for their ancestors, they spoke of nothing but the scandal. How was it possible, they asked, that a holy man of God could forsake everything and go to live in a brothel? They complained to the priest, and demanded that something be done.

The mothers, too, spoke to the priest.

"Our children are young," they said. "They are not wise in the ways of the world. How are we to answer them if they should ask us why it is that a whore and a holy man can live together in our midst? Scandal is being given to our innocent children. You are our priest, our spiritual watchdog. It is your duty to do something."

The priest Nikos had been God's representative in the village ever since the death of the father of Luli Spanakis. Indeed, he had been born in Soros Koprou and had always lived there except during the time he was studying to be a priest. His house and his wife and children and his olive and orange groves and his peanut fields were in Soros Koprou. His life reflected the lives of the villagers and his views reflected their views. He was the fish, and the villagers the water he swam in. Anything that contaminated the water endangered the fish. The priest would have to speak with Luli and with Mikhalis. He would speak with them separately.

He found the monk in the field that sloped steeply down from the rear of the house in the direction of the sea. Mikhalis was pulling up handfuls of weeds. There had been a shower the night before, and the roots yielded easily. Now was the time to pull them, before the rains made them grow stronger and taller, robbing from the soil the moisture needed by the trees.

Mikhalis listened in silence. It was not he, Nikos, who wanted him to go, the priest said. It was the people of the village. It was for their good,

24

and the good of their children, that he was asking Mikhalis in God's name to go back to his cave and remain there.

Mikhalis smiled a bitter smile.

"I know that you must do God's work, Nikos," he said. "In the field I pull out the bad grasses that the trees may have more life and bear better fruit. In God's field you pull out the bad grasses that God's creatures may grow strong without hindrance. I will speak with the daughter of Spanakis."

"I will speak with Luli," the priest said.

She was standing at the door, arms crossed. She had seen him speak with Mikhalis. He greeted her warmly but she eyed him coldly, unspeaking.

"Luli, there is something I want to discuss with you. Do you think we could go in?"

"Wait here," she said, and she went inside. She came out with the axe, closing the door behind her. She stood in front of the door.

"Hypocrite! You have not stood in this house for twenty years, and you will never stand in it again."

"Luli," he began; "I buried your mother. I . . ."

"Hypocrite!" she screamed. "If you try to cross this threshold, before God I swear I will split your rotten skull with this axe! Once before, you gave your advice to me and you gave your advice to Mikhalis and we had to take it, may you be damned! Now we do not want your advice, priest of the Devil. Go away! We will not listen; we will not take your advice."

"Mikhalis will take my advice," the priest said. "Mikhalis is a monk, a holy man. He belongs to God, not to you."

He turned abruptly and walked away. Her voice followed him hoarsely, but he did not turn around.

"May the Devil have you! Mikhalis does not belong to God. He is a man. You will not take him from me."

* * *

Night had spread its black mantle over Soros Koprou. It was mid-November, the time when summer and winter struggled for supremacy, with sometimes one gaining the upper hand, sometimes the other. On this night the advantage lay with winter. The air was chill, the heat of the day only a memory.

Luli and Mikhalis were at their evening meal when the villagers came. They surrounded the house. Only Nikos the priest and the

25

family of Mikhalis were absent. Even the children and the dogs had come.

"Monk, you must leave our village," they said. "Come out now or we will go in and take you out," they shouted, and they hammered with fists on the stout wooden door of the house.

Luli went to the outer room and took up the axe, but Mikhalis took it from her hands.

"It is no use," he said. "In a moment they will break the door and they will take me out. If we fight, they will take me anyway. It is better that we do not fight, for then no harm will come to you or what is yours."

For a moment he looked into the deep, dark eyes that were wet with the tears of fear and anger and love. Then he touched her cheek, opened the door and walked out. The crowd fell silent. "I am leaving," he said. They parted to let him pass, and behind him he heard the low murmur of their voices.

In the morning the house of Luli Spanakis was empty. In the *cafenion* the farmers speculated that perhaps she had eloped with the Mad Monk, but before the sun had set the news came that the monk was alone in his cave. Weeks after, word came that she had been seen, ragged and begging, in a village further along the coast. In January, cold and despair and tiredness and hunger drove her home. The house was just as before. Nothing had been touched. She regained her strength, painted her worn face and went back to her old way of life. A sprinkling of snow lay on the hills above Soros Koprou, and in his cave the Mad Monk Mikhalis shivered and tried to think of God.

In Soros Koprou everything was normal. In the *cafenion* of Dimitrios the farmers passed the time in conversation and in sipping *raki* and Turkish coffee. In the *taverna* of Iorgo the young men met at night to play cards and drink one or two bottles of *ouzo* or beer. The spinsters of the village met in the street, or outside the church on the Holy Day, or at the graveyard where they went to pray for their ancestors. They spoke in low tones, nodding wisely. "A whore is always a whore, and a hermit always a hermit," they said.

The Dollars of Death

The stranger appeared out of the blue one searing hot summer's day and said he was looking for somewhere to stay. It needn't be comfortable but it had to be cheap, he said.

It happened that a man he asked had a small construction firm, and that the firm had offices. That was how it came about that the stranger moved into the offices to share with the caretaker and a young labourer who worked for the company.

The idea was that he would stay a week or so, which was judged time enough for him to find a job and a room of his own. Whenever anyone asked him what kind of a job he was looking for, the stranger shrugged his lean shoulders and said only that he had come to work for the Revolution.

The Revolution was still young in those days and the new administration was only just replacing the shattered skeleton of the old. It wasn't easy to find work for a stranger . . . especially for a pale, silent type from up north who claimed no special qualifications and had no particular work preference.

So it was that the weeks passed and the stranger remained in the offices. None of the people who worked there ever really got to know him; when he wasn't out — which he often was — he sat in a wicker chair out back and read books. Sometimes he read for hours on end without, it seemed to them, moving a muscle.

At first the young office workers thought him very strange. The apprentice accountants would adjust their spectacles and look closely at him from a window or the open door, but his blank expression never changed and he gave no sign that he knew of their attention.

The office girls who typed the letters and the long columns of figures for the apprentice accountants talked in low voices among themselves about the stranger. Some of them thought he was cute; others, that he was just strange. One or two of them felt they were a little in love with him, but these, like the others, he ignored.

After he had been unemployed a month, the owner of the company gave him a job as a helper on the old lorry that ferried blocks and tiles and pipes and cement from the capital to sites far out in the countryside. It was only then that the stranger came out of his shell.

In the cool of the morning while they loaded the lorry he talked to his fellow workers about his country and about what he did there. He told them about his parents and the farm they owned, and about his broken marriage. He told them about his reasons for coming to Latin America, and about his hopes for the future development of the Revolution. In this way, the curiosity of his workmates was all but satisfied.

I say "all but" because there was one thing — a small detail — about the stranger that still baffled them. The mystery had to do with the conspicuous bulge in the right-hand pocket of the bleached, frayed blue jeans he always wore.

Almost from the first day, all had noticed the bulge. At first out of politeness they said nothing, but as soon as they felt they knew him well enough, they asked about it.

But the stranger never answered. Or if he did, it was only to shrug his shoulders and mutter that it was nothing, that it did not concern them.

One or two of the bolder ones said in a voice that was half-serious and half-joking that some day soon they would take hold of him and find out by force what it was that the bulge meant. These the stranger answered only with a slow smile that seemed to say: "You try if you want, my friend, but if you do it is not I who will be responsible for the consequences of your folly." And so the mystery remained.

The two men who every night shared the offices with the stranger wondered about the bulge too. Like most of the questions they asked him, those about the bulge in his pocket went without an answer.

Like their friends who came to the offices at nights and on weekends to drink rum and play cards and dominoes or to listen to the stranger strumming his guitar, they could only guess what the pocket contained. Some believed that it was a holster with a small pistol. Others felt that it was a wallet with personal papers and pictures of loved ones far away. But the general opinion was that the pocket contained dollars.

Once this theory had gained acceptance among them, the question became: "How much?" Anibal, who was without work, and considered an authority on foreigners because he had once had a long affair with a Canadian girl, felt that the stranger probably had only enough dollars to pay his fare back home when the time came.

Eutemio, who was in technical school, said he thought the stranger was rich. The bulge could be any amount of dollars — thousands, even.

28

He could be an agent of the CIA, sent to spy on the Revolution, and only pretending to be poor like them. With foreigners one never knew, he said.

Domingo, who worked in his father's second-hand bookshop, disagreed about the CIA agent bit, but was inclined to agree with Eutemio about the dollars. Had any of them ever seen a *gringo* who was poor? he asked darkly, and all had to agree that indeed they had not seen such a *gringo*.

Rodolfo, the caretaker, was pure indian, and one of those who subscribed to the dollar theory. For many weeks he toyed with the idea of taking the dollars away from the stranger. He would take them one night while the stranger slept and by noon of the same day he could be with his brothers, far away in the countryside.

But in the end he decided against it. He knew that the foreigner slept with a *machete* under the sponge mattress he used as a bed. And who knew what was in the soiled blue rucksack he used as a pillow? A pistol, maybe. Besides, the stranger was a light sleeper, and Rodolfo knew from experience that there was no way to open the door of the office where he slept without waking him.

Juan Carlos slept on the floor, in the carpeted office next to the one used by the stranger. He was black, a descendant of slaves brought to that part of the world by the British to pick cotton. As a labourer, he had less to lose than the caretaker. If he stayed within the law, he would always be a labourer.

Juan Carlos liked women, and he liked to spend money on them, and on himself. For months now he had watched the stranger closely. He had seen how poorly he lived and he had serious doubts about whether the man had any dollars at all. Yet there was a chance that he might have. And in Juan Carlos's view of the universe, a chance was always something to be seized upon.

But caution was needed. He knew about the *machete*, and he knew that the stranger slept more lightly than the mangy cats which at night stalked the waste ground behind the office. By himself, Juan Carlos did not feel equal to the task.

One by one he sounded out the other four, and one by one they voiced their unwillingness. It was unethical, they said, and besides, it was dangerous. There were at that time some forty thousand foreigners in the country, not counting tourists. So far as was known, not a single one of them had been harmed.

There was a feeling among the population — even among the most

29

die-hard enemies of the Revolution — that the foreigners had come to help, and that therefore the least they deserved was to be tolerated. What was more, the foreigners had the reputation of being tough. There were already legends about them, and a certain aura of power or strength surrounded them, so that the natives looked on them in almost the same way that their smooth-faced ancestors had looked on the equally white-faced and equally bearded *conquistadores*.

But if none of his leisure-time friends would help him, Juan Carlos knew someone who would. That someone was Alberto, called *El Cojo* — the lame one. *El Cojo* worked alongside Juan Carlos on the site. His nickname came from his limp, and the limp, like the scars on his once-handsome face, came from his habit of getting into fights.

A lot of things were said about *El Cojo*. So many things were said about him that fact and fiction blended into rumour and legend, so that it was nearly impossible to tell what was true and what was not. But some things everyone knew: the man was ruthless, and his quickness of temper was matched by his speed with a knife.

At lunchtime Juan Carlos took him aside. "Alberto," he said, "Alberto, I need your help as a friend,"and he explained about the stranger with the bulge in the right front pocket of his faded blue jeans.

El Cojo was cautious. He would think it over, he said. As soon as he had made a decision, he would let Juan Carlos know.

For several days he pondered. He knew that he could not afford to take chances. Twice under the old government he had been in jail. The first time was as a teenager, after he had carved a four-inch cut in his father's left cheek with the man's own old-style razor. His mother had called the police.

The second time was some years later when he was already the head of a family. It had been a gang fight, and one of the other side had died. That time *El Cojo*'s stay in prison had been longer. Now with the new government, who knew what might happen if he got in trouble again?

In the end he decided to go ahead with the project. But he would take the stranger alone, in his own time and in his own way, and in a place that he alone would choose. That way, there would be no-one to talk afterwards, and all that the stranger carried would be his.

So he spoke to Juan Carlos. "Let us wait a while longer," he said: "I must make plans."

The next time the lorry came to the site, he limped to where the stranger was unloading cement. "You are welcome in our country,

30

stranger," he said, "I am Alberto. Let us be friends." And *El Cojo* smiled a wide smile, showing a mouth that was half full of gold.

After that whenever the lorry came to the site, Alberto and the stranger spent the free times together, so that the other workers remarked on this odd friendship. Then one Saturday morning when they were unloading bricks together and stacking them beside the lorry, *El Cojo* invited the foreigner to his house.

"My house, it is not much," he said, "but we will be happy to have a visit from you, my wife and I. And I have a *hermanita* — a little sister — living there. I think maybe you will like her. This evening I will come to the office for you, to show you the way that is shortest, so that after, when you go home, you will not lose yourself." And he smiled his wide, gold-plated smile.

The evening was as good as *El Cojo* had promised, except that the stranger didn't much like the little sister. After they had eaten the food prepared by the women, the two men sat outside in wicker chairs and smoked and drank rum. It was long after midnight when they parted: *El Cojo* to go back inside the hut that passed for his home, and the stranger to follow the deserted pathways that would take him quickly back to the offices. There was no human sound, and the night belonged to the plaintive howls of the dogs and the shrill outbursts of the cocks.

* * *

The next morning the stranger shouldered his battered blue rucksack and left the offices as quickly as he had come.

Juan Carlos saw him leaving, and called out to ask him where he went, so early on the morning of Sunday. The stranger paused when he reached the gate. "I go to the airport," he said, and closed the gate.

Four days later when the police found the body at the bottom of a dry well beside a little-used pathway, they knew at once from the scars on the face who it was. The two arms were broken, and a ring of purple-yellow bruises could still be seen on the decomposing flesh of the neck.

Afterwards on a hot night when Rodolfo and Juan Carlos and Anibal and Eutemio and Domingo met as usual outside the offices to watch the girls pass and to while away the time in conversation, the talk was of the strange death of *El Cojo*. Then they talked about the stranger. They would never know now what the bulge had been, they said.

The Moon on The Glacier

Kasper woke because his bladder was full. He did not get up immediately. For several minutes he lay perfectly still in his warm down sleeping bag. Outside the tent, the temperature would be somewhere between minus five and minus ten. The tent was at 13,400 feet, approximately.

At last he had to get up. Dragging his hands out of the tight bag, he undid the cord at the neck and opened the zip half-way down. With his right hand he fumbled for the rubber torch, and found it between the bag and the side of the tent.

He was already wearing his heavy track suit. Now he pulled his boots out of the bottom of the sleeping bag and put them on in the torchlight. He did not tie the laces.

Frank grumbled sleepily when the torch went on, then swore elaborately when Kasper unzipped the flaps. Unlike Kasper, Frank always slept with his head towards the tent entrance. Better air, he said. He wore his balaclava at night.

The snow had stopped. It lay like a sprinkling of talcum powder on the barren, tilted field where the three tents were pitched close together. Just in front of the tent being used by Peter and Hans, a small pool of frozen vomit lay neatly on the snow. In the third tent — the red one that took three people — a light was on. That would be Robert using his head light, studying the information he had about the mountain one more time. Robert was only twenty-four, which made him the third youngest of the seven. But because of his experience of the Himalaya, he was group leader. He shared the tent with the two Japanese, Maeda and Kanda.

"To hell with the mountain," Kasper thought, relieving himself. It was the glacier that worried him. The glacier came first. If they got over that, the peak itself would be a pleasure, in spite of the cold. He was a fairly experienced rock climber, but knew little about ice.

As he made his way back towards the tents the cloud broke and suddenly a perfect moon hung like a silver lamp over the glacier. Here and there, stars showed through rents in the dissipating cloud cover. An enchanted light flooded the mountainside.

A new mood took possession of Kasper. He no longer felt like sleeping. He wanted to partake of this enchantment, to breathe it in, to live it now. For the first time since awakening, he looked at his watch. It was 9.30. That meant he could only have slept for less than an hour. He returned to the tent and shuffled into the bulky down jacket he had been using as a pillow. Then he took the waterproof trousers from his rucksack, kicked his boots off, and sat on the sleeping bag to put the trousers on as extra protection against the cold. He switched the torch off and left it in the tent. He put the boots on, took his two-litre plastic water bottle, crawled out of the tent, did the flaps, and tied the boot laces. Though his lips were raw and bleeding, he whistled as he walked down the trail to the village.

On his map the village was called Karamcha. On Robert's, it was called Larumchok. The village was a single stone house, built of the same loose grey rocks that littered the steep slope between the house and the river.

Just in front of the house he left the track and began the scramble down to the river. It would be frozen on top, but he could easily put a boot through the ice and fill the bottle. In the dry mountain air it was important to drink enough. Drinking enough meant drinking more than you felt like drinking.

"If you want water, you may have it from our house; the river has become frozen," said a woman's voice behind him. Kasper was so startled that he stopped in his tracks. Then, very slowly, he turned around. Above him on the trail he saw an oldish woman in the traditional wool and sheepskin garb of the mountain folk.

He retraced his steps. His heartbeats were like hammer blows, partly from the effort of climbing the slope and partly from the shock the woman had caused him. He had heard that the people in these parts went to bed with the sun. Certainly he would not have expected to meet anybody nearly three hours after nightfall. But to be addressed in fluent English was the biggest surprise. Here in these remote stone mountains, where the terrain was so rough and access over the high passes so difficult that the people did not even have the wheel, to be spoken to out of the darkness by a local woman in English was almost like meeting an alien fresh off a spaceship.

And yet his surprises were only beginning. It was to be a night of surprises. As soon as he reached the track he looked again at the

33

woman, and his heart beat faster than ever. She was not at all old, but quite young — mid-twenties, perhaps. And even in the moonlight he could see that she was very beautiful. He followed her inside, his mind full of confusion, his brain rehearsing a dozen eager questions.

In a bare stone room dimly lit by a single kerosene lamp she took a blue or green plastic jug and broke the thin ice on a blue or green plastic pail of water. He held the bottle for her, but his hand trembled and she smiled and took it from him and filled it herself. Then she replaced the stopper and screwed the cap back on and smiled again and handed him the bottle.

"Your English is very good," he said lamely, fingering the bottle. She laughed, and her laugh was like music. "I have been educated a little," she said. "First in Srinagar. Public school. Afterwards at university, in London. You are from Britain?"

"The United States, " Kasper said. "I am Irish-American." At that moment he fervently wished he were from London. But as a student he had worked there during several long, hot summers, for he had passed through an Irish university upon the insistence of his Irish mother, and spent summers with her brother in Cricklewood. They had, therefore, much to talk about. It even turned out that they lived in London at the same time, and within two miles of each other.

She was eager to talk, for now she rarely had the opportunity to use her English. The more he listened, and the more he looked into the dark, intense pools of her eyes and admired the thick, blue-black hair and the finely-chiselled Tibetan features and the healthy glow of her brown skin, the more completely fascinated he grew.

The money for her education had come from two older brothers in the U.S. They had a small timber business in Connecticut. They would have liked her to join them; with her good English they could use her as a secretary, not to mention a housekeeper, since neither was married. But her father would not leave the village. Her father *was* the village. He was an old man of nearly seventy, and he clung to the old ways. He grew his own barley and made his own *chang* from it and drank it alone or with whatever travellers happened to stop in the village. He threshed his own grain, tying his yaks together in a short, shaggy row to the smooth wooden pole fixed in the centre of the circular threshing floor at the side of the house and singing to them as he walked them endlessly round and round so that their hooves separated golden grain from golden straw.

Now the harvest time was over. Already the hay was stored on the roof and the winter supply of grain was ready for the making of the big, round cakes of Tibetan bread that — with rice, *dal*, barley, flour and tea — would be their food for the winter.

The old man was asleep, wrapped in a thick, dusty blanket in the next room. A great shortness of breath afflicted him now, and his eyes were growing dim. He might live a month, or a year, or ten years. But he would die in his own house in his own village in the dry, barren mountains that were the only place he knew. And until he died, he needed his one surviving daughter, his little Tashi.

Kasper took the butter tea she offered him, and drank it greedily. She gave him *chang*, and he drank that too, and looked at her while she slowly sipped her tea. Together they sat on a thick wool blanket by the small wood and dung fire — small, for wood was precious in these mountains, and collected by her far afield in a wicker basket carried on her back. Her father gathered the dung nearer home. She wrapped herself in a blanket and gave him another, and they talked and grew closer as the night progressed.

When they had talked long about London, they spoke a little about the United States: how he knew it to be, and how she imagined it to be. Then he told her about Ireland. After that, she talked to him about Ladakh, of which he knew little, having come up from Srinagar on the bus less than a week earlier.

He told her of their plans for the mountain, and she grew worried. "Kasper," she said, "you and your friends, you must not be foolish. Really, the climbing season is quite over. It was ended before the harvest. Even the trekking usually ends by early October, and already we are near to November." Inwardly, he agreed. But he kept this feeling to himself. They had been aware of the risks when they took the decision in Srinagar to attempt the mountain. It had been too late then to seek permission. That would have taken three weeks. Anyway, there was nobody around to check whether or not they had permits. Their mountain was not in the restricted zone, so the military wouldn't bother them. If the weather held, they could do it. So far, the weather was holding.

Still, Kasper was uneasy, his apprehension reawakened by the girl's words. Without permission, there would be hell to pay if an accident happened. All they could do then would be to plead ignorance. And that might not be easy, given that Robert knew the Great Himalayan Range well, and the two Japanese had clambered all over the Karakorams.

Partly out of curiosity, but mainly to ease his mind, he shifted the talk back to more intimate things. Was there a boyfriend? he asked.

There was, she admitted shyly. In a village further up the valley, about a dozen kilometers away. The village was Zindon, and her fiancé's name was Migyur.

Migyur was a soldier — already an officer, in fact. He was on border duty deep in the restricted zone, stationed with his unit high up among the peaks and glaciers of the Karakoram. In the spring he would return, most likely with a new promotion, and then they would be married. She would remain in the village while her father lived. She would see her new husband during leave periods. Afterwards, when her father passed on, they would be together in married quarters.

Then the village would die? In a way it would, she said. Father wanted the elder son, Dorjee, to return and carry on the tradition but he merely deluded himself, for there was no chance of either son returning to these mountains to live. But the village would remain as a place where goatherds stopped with their flocks during the long journeys to and from the high mountain pastures. Goats and sheep and ponies and the sturdy little Ladakh donkeys would shelter where they now sat drinking *chai* and *chang*.

Seeing his concerned look, she tossed her glossy mane and laughed. "Please, you must not worry. Who could have expected such sadness in the face of a mountaineer? All these things are far away in the future. For the nearer time, father and I have other problems to think upon, for we must face the long, hard winter really without a man."

He searched her eyes for a hint of playfulness, but she looked back at him intently. He had told her he meant to remain six months in Ladakh and that, after the mountain, he was without specific plans. There was a silence — the longest since the conversation began, hours earlier.

She laughed again — a little nervously this time, he thought. "You know that here in the mountains we have our customs," she said. "Often it happens that two brothers will marry the one wife. Among us it is accepted. Of course this will not be my case. Even my poor Migyur will not come until April.

"Father wishes for a man in the house. If not one of my brothers, then my Migyur. And if not he either, then some man at least, for we are weak, Father and I, and the animals must be tended in the cold times."

"Even a foreigner?" Kasper said. She laughed. "Yes, a foreigner even. Men are men, after all is said. But of course, he would have to be good with the animals who in winter live with us in this house. And strong. Like some mountain climber, I think."

It was his turn to laugh. "My uncle has a farm in Maryland. I spent a lot of time there as a child. No dzos or yaks, mind you, but I do know something about cattle." She looked him straight in the eye. "You are a city boy," she said. "I am afraid one winter in these mountains would kill you."

"Don't tempt me," he said.

She refilled her cup. "Oh, but I want to tempt you. As I already have explained, Father and I must have a man in the winter."

"Your father would kill me."

"No," she said. "Father would, I am sure, make you most welcome. Even if he made a problem, you could show him some money, and promise it for the spring to him. Father puts great importance in rupees."

He drained his cup of *chang* and refilled it, slowly and deliberately, from the bottle marked "Rum: Indian Army Issue." When he looked at her again, there was a twinkling of mischievous challenge in his eyes. "All right, city woman. If your father asks me, I will stay. So now who's bluffing?"

"Soon after it lightens he will rise, and I will ask him," she said, her gaze unflinching. They talked of other things, now seriously, now playfully.

In time her father rose, and she introduced them. The old man wore a soiled baggy robe the colour of old straw, tied around the waist with a purple sash. Kasper guessed that the garment was made from old sacking. Father's face was creased and burned by the mountain sun, and when he took the visitor's hand he held it long in a firm grip and squinted at him with eyes that were as tiny slits cut by some careless awl in crinkled leather.

Holding Kasper's hand between his calloused palms, the old man spoke at great length in Ladakhi. Kasper was embarrassed. His eyes sought Tashi's, pleading for an interpretation. But she was silent until her father had done.

"Father invites you to pass the winter with us," she said simply then.

Kasper withdrew his hand from the old man's grasp. He looked at Tashi, but she turned away and busied herself with kitchen tasks. Kasper's throat was dry, and his head swam. It was, he told himself, the altitude. That and his tiredness. He went to the door and, propping himself against the weatherbeaten jamb, looked long at the mountain.

37

It was still in shadow. Never had he seen a mountain look so cold, inhospitable, uninviting.

He felt the old man's hand on his shoulder. Food was ready. Together the three ate *chapatis, tsampa* and small boiled eggs, and washed it all down with strong butter tea of the kind drunk in the region of Tibet. When the meal was eaten, Kasper shook the old man's hand. Then he exchanged a long and wordless look with the woman, and left. From the doorway she called him, and came hurrying out with the water bottle he had forgotten. She knew that no decision had been made.

"While you are at your climbing, you may think of your plan for winter," was all she said.

When he got back to the tents, Frank was still asleep, but the others were busy around a small breakfast fire. He squatted beside them and took a long draught from his water bottle. Robert looked at him quizzically.

"We were discussing the climb," he said. "You know there's a lot of homework still to be done. How do you feel about the whole thing now?"

Kasper didn't answer. His mind was not on the mountain. Now his thoughts wandered back to the time, many hours before, when he had seen the moon on the glacier. He stood up suddenly and went to wake Frank.

Shots in The Night

It was night in the forest. There was no moon and the stars were pinpricks of light, outshone by the fireflies.

A young man was slowly climbing a hill on the dirt track that was called a road because here there was no other. His walk was weary, and the strap of the heavy rucksack he carried bit through the sweat-soaked cotton of his shirt and into the flesh of his shoulder. Wet red earth clung to his boots and deadened the sound of his footsteps. There was no sound except the eternal insect noise of the forest, and Robert — for that was the young man's name — had long since ceased to hear it.

At the top of the hill he paused and shifted the weight of the rucksack from the sore place. Below him in the distance he could see the lights of the camp at La Rosita. At the bottom of the ravine he made out the shape of the river, its surface like a crinkled grey ribbon in the faintness of the starglow. Its width surprised him and he wondered if he would be able to cross, because of course there would not be a bridge.

But the lights from the camp encouraged him, and he quickened his downhill step. He had been walking since dawn. In the morning he had crossed the flooded Wanlí in the dugout canoe of an old indian. The other rivers had been shallow, with stony bottoms, and he had crossed them on foot. He had walked fast and steadily, eating dry salty biscuits from a plastic bag, and stopping only three times to ask for a glass of water in the palm-thatch huts of the indians. It was the start of the rainy season and already on this road nothing could move except the powerful road-building machines of the Cubans who lived in the camp at La Rosita.

When he reached the river, he stopped and surveyed the opposite bank. Near the water, in the shade of some Ceiba trees, he distinguished the faint whiteness of the big tents where the Cubans slept. Further from the river, at the other side of the clearing, were the oblong wooden buildings where the lights were and that served as canteen, storeroom and repair sheds. In the centre of the clearing, between the tents and the wooden buildings, he could see the outlines of the tractors and lorries and the other earth-moving machines, parked in rows. To his left, further along the river-bank, was the cluster of huts known as the village of La Rosita.

Directly across from where he was standing, the dirt track emerged from the river to climb again into the forest, with the clearing to the left of it. Near the edge of the clearing, between the track and the oblong wooden buildings, a tall, shadowy figure was walking.

Robert Brown waited until the militiaman reached the water's edge. Then he called out to him, hoping that he would not be startled by the shout.

"Good night, *compañero*," he said. "The river here — how is it?" The militiaman had seen him, and answered without surprise, his fingers resting lightly on the short barrel of the Uzi which hung by a strap from his shoulder.

"It flows fast, but it is not very deep; you can cross," he said. Robert hoisted the rucksack onto his shoulder and, holding it with both hands, crossed slowly beside the steel skeleton of what would soon be a bridge. In the centre the current was swift and the cold mountain water came almost to his armpits.

He came out shivering and with the water squelching in his boots. Setting the rucksack down, he took out a crumpled packet of cigarettes. Taking one himself and offering the tall youth another, he began the explanation he knew the militiaman was waiting for. The Nicaraguan listened without interrupting.

"Go to the first tent and ask for Raúl; there is a mattress," he said when Robert had finished. Robert took the rucksack and limped towards the tent.

"Wait," the militiaman said: "You will have hunger." He pointed. "The canteen is over there. Ask for Humberto . . . say Julio sent you."

He had emptied the tin tray of rice, beans, meat and soup and was talking to some of the workers who had come back late when the militiaman motioned him to come outside.

"*Compañero*," he said: "If you like, you can go to your tent now. Not everyone here is Cuban. There are some who do not like the *internacionalistas* . . . there are bad people. You do not need to answer their questions. Here you must be careful."

They shook hands for the second time that night. The militiaman smiled: "I hope you sleep well. Tomorrow, in the morning, there will be lorries going to Palma Mocha, and from there there will be much traffic. That you may have a good journey."

* * *

40

Robert Brown woke suddenly and sat up. It was pitch dark in the tent. Anxiety made his head clear, his senses instantly alert. His ears disentangled the sounds of the night. From within, the snoring of the workers. From without, the murmur of the river, the shrill clamour of the forest insects and, far away, the roaring of a puma — the animal the indians called *el tigre*. He lit a match and looked at the waterproof watch. It was 1.40.

Then he heard the sound that had awakened him. The single sharp crack of a rifle, echoed by the rocks of the riverbank. Fumbling for the rucksack, he unzipped a side pocket and pulled out the .38. Quickly and silently he slipped out of the tent, pushing the revolver into the pocket of his already-dry jeans.

He found the militiaman crouched, Uzi in hand, behind a tree at the edge of the river. Robert touched the youth's shoulder.
"Are you the only one?" he asked.
"Do not worry; all here have guns."
"But are there other *milicianos?*" the European asked.
"In the village — enough," the Latin American whispered. "Wait. They will come."
"Do you have . . . trouble here often?"
"Not this; never," the militiaman said. He turned and sat with his back to the tree, his head resting lightly against the bark, the gun between his knees. "It's a Fal," he said: "You can always tell. I was in the mountains . . . fourteen months. In the north. Las Segovias."
"Like Sandino," the other said. The sound of the rifle came again, and the rocks answered. Robert shivered and fingered the revolver in his pocket. Another shot, and the metallic ring of bullet on stone.
"*Gringo*, are you afraid?" the youth asked, looking up without shifting his position.
"Yes," Robert Brown said: "I am afraid." The militiaman leaned the stock of the submachine gun on the ground and grasped the barrel with both hands. "You must not have fear," he said. "War is like with women . . . like sex. A man can live without knowing it, and when it comes he can be afraid. But this fear is no good. A man must do the best he can with a war, like with a woman."
"You are safe here, *gringo*. This Fal, if he is only one, then there is no problem. We will find him. In a day, or a week, or in two weeks, or in a month. The indians will tell us where he is."
"And if there are many?"
"Give me a cigarette," the militiaman said. "Even if there are many,

41

they cannot take us here. At night they cannot see us. If they try to cross the river, or to come by the road, we will take them all. In daylight, they have no chance.

Along the riverbank, silent men with rifles were moving under the trees. Some had come from the huts in the village, others from the big white tents. A short man with a heavy mustache spoke in low, quick Spanish.

"They have called Palma Mocha," the militiaman said more slowly. "There is an army post. They do not think that there is a counter-revolutionary band within a hundred kilometres of here."

"But this man with the Fal . . . ," Robert said.

"He is alone. A madman with a gun in the night. Like an animal roaring. An enemy of the people, of our Revolution. . . a hater of our internationalist brothers. Relax, *gringito*. We will find this animal, and we will cage him, like the mountain people do with *el tigre* when he is young, to tame him.

"At dawn there is a truck to Palma Mocha. You can go with it. The *capitán* will go too, to make a report.

"Sleep, *gringo*. If he comes, this animal of the mountain, we will kill him."

Murphy

Murphy was enjoying himself. His eardrums vibrated with the mindless midwestern music of the Arapahoes showband, fed electronically into the two vast banks of amplifiers standing one on either side of the stage and facing the packed dance-hall. A pall of cigarette smoke hung in the rancid air above the heads of the sweating multitude, fed by little rivulets of smoke from hundreds of cigarettes, one of which belonged to Murphy — his twelfth of the night.

The music stopped and there was a brief respite before it began again. Murphy drained the last of his whiskey and set the glass down on the bar counter. Then he joined the heaving, sweating wave of frustrated males in the surge across the polished wooden floor towards where the women stood in ill-defined rows, like the cast-off shells of molluscs on a sea-shore.

Murphy was short — only five feet two inches — and his fat neck strained to lift the massive head just high enough for him to see in shadowy outline, over the shoulders of those in front, the forms of the front ranks of females. These he perceived with some difficulty in the half-light of the lurid red and purple bulbs set far above him in the ceiling, and which only dimly penetrated the numbing alcoholic fog already enshrouding his brain. Little drops of sweat glistened individually on the red meat of his neck and occasionally one trickled down onto the frayed cotton collar of his once-white, open shirt, adding to the ring of moisture where collar touched skin.

Murphy hardly noticed the sweat, which caused him no more discomfort than the unmistakable stench of mingled farts and perfume which pervaded the hall. Though he used his considerable bulk to shoulder and push his way through the throng, the opening number of the set was already far advanced when he reached the rows of women, thinned now by the temporary departure of those who had accepted dances.

The human tide happened to disgorge him at a point where two frail and worn-looking spinsters in their late thirties stood in almost dignified apprehension. Murphy looked them up and down, then

43

jerked his head and rolled his hurting eyeballs in the direction of the dance-floor. The sisters averted their offended eyes, and he moved on down the line, meeting a succession of refusals, which were accompanied in the cases of some of the younger women by derisive laughter.

Presently the wave abated and Murphy heaved himself back through the random motion of dancing couples to the bar. He pushed his way to the counter, ordered a whiskey and a pint of Guinness, then stood with his back to the bar while he watched the progress of the dance. He was enjoying himself immensely.

It was St. Patrick's Night, and the band had been imported from Ireland specially for the occasion. On other nights, touring Irish country and western bands were used. In all other respects, the proceedings closely resembled those of a normal week-end dance in the Auld Country club. The packed attendance was perhaps slightly larger than was customary. The five pounds admission price was par for the course. So too was the presence of bouncers — burly men of early middle age clad in dark dinner suits and matching bow ties, the only difference being that tonight there were seven instead of the normal five.

In all the many Irish dance-halls throughout London, the same scene was being enacted. These halls had names like the Macushla Club, the Molly Malone, the Gra mo Chroi and the Mainland — all names, like that of the Auld Country club itself, which evoked memories of Ireland in the minds of the Irish exiles who read the dance-hall advertisements in the Irish Post, which conveniently reached the shops on Thursday, though datelined the following Saturday.

In each of these halls on this Friday night on March 17th, perhaps a quarter of the attendance was made up of couples. About a third of the remainder were women, and two-thirds men. A good proportion of these unattached women were well into their thirties, and many were even older. They stood passively around three sides of the hall, the fourth being where the stage was. Despite the experience to the contrary accumulated over years and even decades, all had come in hopes of meeting the Prince Charming who would take them out onto the dance-floor and, ultimately, out of the dreary grind of life as a factory worker, barmaid or hotel skivvy and into that blissful and sanctified state known as Holy Matrimony, for all these women were Roman Catholics. In this forlorn hope did most of them endure the weekly, twice weekly, or even thrice weekly indignity of these flesh markets, like so many cows and heifers at a cattle fair.

The buyers were the men. Their superiority in numbers was a result of the lop-sided structure of Irish emigration during the previous decades, and a cause of that form of primal competition which sent them surging across the dance-floor in periodic waves in the desperate quest for a partner. A goodly number were drunk. They were drunk in part because, while they earned what could be described as decent wages — often in the construction industry — they lacked the elementary cultural education which would have disposed them towards a more rational and less personally harmful manner of spending their hard-earned money. But they were drunk mainly because, without the venomous liquid which they deposited in their bellies and which seeped into their bloodstreams, they found themselves incapable of making the requisite amorous advances towards the opposite sex.

The consequences of such alcoholic dependence were several. In the first place it meant that, while the spirit or the Guinness was willing, the flesh was weak, so that in the tiny percentage of cases where liaisons were actually formed, nothing concrete generally came of it. Of more general relevance was the fact that it reduced those who consumed it in excess to slobbering imbeciles, thereby degrading not only the intoxicated themselves, but also the objects of their lust, who had to submit to their leering, lecherous looks, slurred invitations to dance, and the insults which sometimes accompanied refusals.

About half-an-hour after midnight, Murphy abandoned the quest and devoted the remaining hour of the dance to the consumption of whiskey and Guinness on a one-for-one basis. Then the metal grill of the bar shutters came down, the band departed the stage and the patrons began to leave in couples, or in small groups, or singly. Not all were yet ready to forsake the sticky warmth of the club, however. Several lingered in little knots scattered around the dance-floor, on the balcony, and especially near the exits.

Murphy was one of those who did not leave. He was looking for Willie, with whom he had begun the evening in the public bar of the Iron Maiden. They had come to the dance together in a taxi and had continued their drinking at the bar until Willie decided to try his luck with the women. Murphy strained his bloodshot eyes as he plodded flat-footed from group to group, hazily reflecting that his younger friend and workmate had probably taken himself off with some young thing again, though in truth Willie with a few drinks on board was not fastidious about the age of his conquests, despite his youth and relative good looks.

At last he found him on the near-deserted balcony, talking with three others, one of whom he recognised as Willie's brother. The other two were strangers. "Naira bit a skirt?" Murphy asked rhetorically as he sidled up to the group, adding in a deep voice when the other shook his head: "Begod we must be failin'; either that or the wimmin is gettin' scarce."

They detached themselves from the others and were about to leave when Murphy saw the woman sitting at one of the small round tables arranged in a row along the dais at the front of the balcony. They ambled over for a closer look. A definitive decision regarding the quality of the merchandise was made difficult by the layer of make-up caking the forty-year-old face, and by the lack of white light.

Willie stood wide-legged, hands in trouser pockets, beside the table. He was looking quizzically at his friend, who by this time had plopped heavily down on to the chair opposite the beautiful hag. Murphy propped his elbows wearily on the white vinyl table top that was wet with beer. He inserted his head between chunky hands and stared intently at the woman on the other side of the table, meanwhile slowly running thick, nicotined fingers through well-clipped, curly, black hair.

"Hello luv," he said: "All alone are ya?" Despite the enormous quantity of beer, now laced with whiskey and Guinness as it swilled around the great vat that was his belly, and despit the fire in his brain, he spoke in a slow, measured way and the words came out distinctly.

The false brunette smiled a crinkled smile, ignoring the blast of fetid air that emerged from between two columns of straight but semi-rotten teeth to accompany Murphy's words across the table.

"I am," she said, "but it's how I want to be. Is he with you?" she added, after a somewhat superficial examination of Willie. Before Murphy could reply, Willie intervened.

"Ah, come on Murphy, fer Chris' sakes. We'll do no good here tonight, an tamarra's ony Sathurday y'know."

"Fuck tamarra," Murphy said, but he levered himself with difficulty out of the low chair and followed his friend from the hall.

At twenty-eight, Willie was eight years younger than Murphy, though in many ways his experience of living was broader. He had been married at twenty-one, and had a wife and two daughters in the northwest of Ireland. The couple were now separated and had not seen each other for more than two years, though for tax purposes Willie conserved the fiction that he was a man with great family responsibilities.

His work experience likewise exceeded that of his best friend. He had started his working life as a helper in a delivery van, before learning the trade of motor mechanic, at which he worked in the town where he was born, before and after his marriage. Then the emigrant boat had taken him to Britain, to work on building sites in Newcastle, Liverpool, Birmingham, Bristol and finally London, where three years before, he had turned his labouring skills for the first time to the civil engineering side of the construction industry.

Murphy's work experience, though longer, was confined to menial tasks as a teenager working for local farmers in the Irish east midlands, followed by nearly two decades as a labourer in London, almost all of that time having been spent with the well-known Irish firm of P. Dempsey and Sons.

Dempsey himself came from the same part of rural Ireland and the same small farming background. He had come to London between the wars, with much less than a pound in his pocket, leaving a widowed mother and five young brothers and sisters behind him. Two older brothers had taken the boat before him. For a long time now, nothing had been heard of Jack, the elder of the two. Some said he died in a nursing home of cancer, others that he had enlisted and been killed in the War, and still others that the drink had killed him in Birmingham or Manchester, but nobody really knew.

Larry, the second brother, worked for over twenty years as a foreman with his younger brother's firm, before returning in the late nineteen sixties to buy a small farm in Munster and live out his days in peace. Murphy had worked under him on the last job he supervised before retiring and had found him a sour and silent man, taking little interest in those who worked under him as long as they did what was expected of them. Patrick Dempsey himself, known to all who worked for him as "Oul Dempsey," had been dead for many years now. But he had left an empire behind him: an empire that still bore his name and was run, and largely owned, by his own two sons.

Oul Paddy was well thought of now, though Murphy knew that such had not always been the case when he was alive. He had been a hard man, but fair, the labourers said when they remembered him in conversation; a man who never refused a fellow countyman a job if he could use him at all. Even today, the firm was full of Tipperary and Kilkenny men, though of course there were men from other parts of Ireland too, and a sprinkling of lorry drivers, labourers and engineers from England, with even a black face here and there.

Murphy had always admired Oul Dempsey, though of course he had never actually spoken to him. A man who had come over like himself without a bob to his name to begin with pick and shovel and who had ended up with twelve hundred men taking the orders from him had to be a great man. And his success was all the more noteworthy because it had been accomplished, not among his own people, but in England.

Murphy did not pause in an attempt to analyse the conjunction of social, economic and political circumstances and personal character traits that had made such success a reality. For him, success had come to Oul Dempsey not because he had slaved and scraped and saved to buy his first primitive, battered earth-shifting lorry, then by an adroit mixture of cunning, careful management, cheating and currying favour had been ideally placed to take full advantage of the post-war construction boom at a time when English cities contained massive mounds of shattered masonry and miles of mangled gas pipes and electricity cables and when the country was crying out for more and better roads. Nor had he built his empire on the strained, arthritic backs of his less competent and more scrupulous fellow Irishmen. No. As far as Murphy was concerned, Oul Paddy died a millionaire because he was a great bloody man, an' that was all that was to it.

Outside the Auld Country club, they looked for a taxi, but the odd one that came had always been ordered by somebody else, and there was a queue in the mini-cab office opposite the club.

"Curse a God on them anyway; they'd be runnin' a man down in the street if he didn't want wan," Murphy growled.

"Sure we'll walk; c'mon, it's only a mile," Willie said. Each turned his jacket collar up and they began to walk briskly, open-necked and coatless, heads bent against the thickening drizzle. It was just after two a.m., and work began at eight.

After Willie left him, Murphy continued along the sodden, near-deserted High Road, stopping only at the Yangtze Takeaway, from which local establishment he emerged a quarter of an hour later, clutching a plain brown paper bag. Then he turned a corner and plodded up a dark hill that climbed wearily between low walls of faded yellow brick, to exhaust itself as soon as it met the street where Murphy lived now and where he had lived for the last fourteen years, having moved only once since he came to London.

Melrose Avenue lay in the heart of what had once been a mecca of clean, quiet, respectable, solid living: an area of neat red-brick houses with well-kept gardens that the English middle class had been proud to call its own. But the executives, factory managers, civil servants and schoolteachers and their wives and children had gone now, to live in tree-lined avenues further north, or in bright new industrial towns. Most of those who ran the string of little shops spoke to each other in strange oriental languages, and many were the black and brown faces in the streets. And on the chipped brick of the wall just around the corner from where Murphy lived was written in white chalk letters a metre high, the legend "I.R.A."

Only in exceptional cases did the houses belong to those who lived in them. The majority were rented by brown-skinned Indians or Pakistanis and black-skinned West Indians and sallow-skinned Greeks and white-skinned Irish. The Indians and Pakistanis and West Indians and Greeks and Irish rented whole houses and half houses and individual rooms, and halves of rooms that had once been large single rooms but now were two small rooms.

The whole houses and halves of houses and individual rooms and halves of rooms were rented to them by the owners, who also happened very often to be brown-skinned Indians or Pakistanis, or black-skinned West Indians, or sallow-skinned Greeks, or white-skinned Irish. All of whom, like Murphy himself, had come to Britain with nothing. But unlike Murphy, they now prided themselves on being in a position to offer a valuable and necessary service to their respective fellow-countrymen who had nothing and who, if the generous landlords had any say in the matter, would in all probability continue to have nothing.

Murphy fumbled his key in the lock of the white hall door with number forty-seven on top, then climbed the stairs to the big room that served him as bedroom, sitting room and kitchen. The bedsitter was spacious and amply furnished, and Murphy considered it well worth the thirty pounds a week he paid for it. Like the double-leafed table which stood between the window and the four-ringed electric cooker in the corner, the room bore the imprint of several days untidiness, and this recent untidiness overlay a much longer period of benign neglect.

He pushed an assortment of unwashed culinary objects towards the centre of the table and wiped the breadcrumbs and sugar grains from the exposed area with a sweep of his left hand before setting the brown bag down. He washed a greasy dinner plate under the cold tap in the sink, wiped it with a damp blue j-cloth that was almost as greasy, and took the two cardboard containers out of the paper bag. On the plate he mixed the rice from one of the containers with the chicken portions and the thick sauce from the second. After washing the feast down with the curdling contents of a half-empty milk bottle, he set the battered alarm clock for a quarter past six, peeled off jacket, trousers, shoes and socks, and went to bed in his underwear and shirt. He slept at once.

He dreamt of black, big-breasted mermaids sporting in an Irish lake.

The Flight from Miami

The lean brown man sprawled in the window seat of the plane with his body twisted sideways away from the window. He drew hard on the cigar in his mouth and looked at the fat white man dozing in the window seat opposite.

It was nine years since they had met, but when he had seen him in the departure lounge, he had known at once that this was the man. He looked a decade older and a stone fatter and a bit balder than before, but there was no mistaking the insolence in the bulging grey eyes, or the way the jowels hung, or the strange, swinging, sideways motion of the body when he walked.

But he had not introduced himself, and, of course, the other had not recognised him. The brown man had changed a good deal in nine years. At twenty-eight, he was heavier and more mature, and the short-sleeved cotton shirt, patched blue jeans and army surplus boots had long since been replaced by tailored shirt and trousers and polished brown shoes. Only one thing had not changed at all. The hatred he carried within him for this white man had not changed. It could never change, no matter how many years might pass.

The cabin signs advising passengers not to smoke and to fasten seat belts came on. The lean brown man stubbed his cigar out and watched the fat white man who was thirty years older fumble with the buckle on his seat belt. In fifteen minutes they would be on the only runway of the *Aeropuerto Internacional Joaquin Gonzalez.*

He remembered the last time, which was also the first, that he had looked out of an aircraft window and seen the same row of sandy, scrub-stubbled hills. He had been nineteen then, just out of High School, and with a burning sense of what was just and what was unjust, born out of the television pictures that came back from Vietnam and the turmoil that raged in the streets and on the campuses of the great North American cities.

His had been the third relief plane to land at the airport, which that time had borne the name of the father of the general who was then the ruler of the country. The first two planes had landed the evening before

51

his, within hours of the airport being re-opened, two days after the earthquake had shattered the city. Both of these first two planes had been Cuban. While he was still in the terminal building he had watched them take off again, still fully laden with the medicines, tents and relief workers brought from Havana. The General had decided that those of his people who were still alive did not want the help of the Communists.

He had come in a cargo plane from Miami, because that was where he happened to be at the time and because he knew the captain slightly and because he knew how to invent medical qualifications and back them up with the verbal fervour of a fiery idealism. It was two weeks later that he met Julie. By then the last of the smoke from the disaster fires had been wafted away by the winds which blew from the lake, the last of the putrefying bodies had been wrenched from the wreckage, and the bulldozers had moved in to level what remained of the crumbling shells that had once been houses, offices, factories and shops.

They had met in one of the tent cities that had sprung up on the new wasteland of the destroyed capital. Like him, she had been helping in an emergency vaccination campaign that was trying to halt the ravages of the tropical diseases that had come with the earthquake. Unlike him, the qualifications she had were real ones. Even clad in oversized rags, to her knees in the yellow mud of the tent site, and wan-faced with the exhaustion of her work, she had appeared particularly beautiful. Hers had not been the cosmetic beauty of the dance floor, or even the beauty of unblemished skin. It had been beauty of a different kind: a beauty that was of looks, but yet only partly of looks, because it depended too on a kind of serenity born of an unshakeable belief that she was where she should be, doing what she should be doing.

They had been together for only nine days, but long before the end of that time he had known that he loved her. It had seemed as if the long hours of their work, far from separating them, only bound them more closely together. They would remain in Nuevo Laredo. She would work in a hospital, and he would teach English; if not in a school, then privately, to anyone who wanted to learn. The jobs would not matter. They would be together.

But their dream had been shattered, and it was far beyond repair. He remembered the day the fat white man had come with another in a jeep to claim his daughter, and he remembered how she had pleaded with him to be allowed to stay with the man and the work that she loved. He remembered her hot tears two days later in the terminal as she waited for the scheduled Nuevo Laredo Airlines flight that went to San Salvador and from there to Miami. The fat white man had not even bothered to come and see her off; had not allowed her to wait the extra two days while he completed his business, so that she could return home the way she had come — in her father's private Twin Otter.

The man had never seen his daughter again. The old propeller-driven aircraft had skidded on touchdown on the runway of San Salvador Airport, wet after a recent rain-shower. Three of the forty-two people on board had died instantly when the wing of a parked military plane tore a hole in the fuselage. Two more had died the next day in hospital, and she had been the first of the two.

And so the fat man had returned to his bitter wife in his private plane. After long negotiations with the representatives of the General, he had the contract he sought. Signatures had been exchanged, and the three Nuevo Laredo pharmaceutical companies — all of which were in part owned by the General — had committed themselves to doing business with the great drug manufacturer whose agent had come with a crocodile-skin briefcase half full of dollars.

At first the brown youth had thought about suicide. Later he had joined a small peasant guerrilla group in the mountains, not caring whether death came to claim him. Death claimed others, but not him. They smuggled him wounded across the border to the north, and when he was well enough he went overland to the United States and began the law studies he had been considering twenty-two months before.

Now he followed the older white man slowly down the steps of the plane and across the sun-bleached tarmac to the glass-fronted terminal building. He knew why the other had come. To sell something. To sell something to the new Revolutionary Government.

To the white man, the nature of the regime he was dealing with was of no interest; he had dealt with every kind of regime. What mattered was that there had been a disaster, and after a disaster, business opportunities always presented themselves. To the fat white man, the Revolution, like the earthquake nine years before, was simply a disaster. A lot of people had died and, more significantly, a lot of property had been damaged and a lot of things were in short supply.

Now the fat man waited while a customs official checked the twin leather suitcases he carried. He waited a long time. The lean brown man spent this time chatting in fluent Spanish to an airport employee. Then he chose a particular customs official, greeted him as a very old friend, and passed through with only a cursory check of his bags.

53

Outside, he noted the number of the licence plate on the back of the taxi which the fat white man had just hired. He took a blue-covered notebook from an inside pocket and wrote down the information. Then he walked back inside the terminal building, to where the telephones were.

He dialled one of the numbers that he knew corresponded to the Ministry of the Interior, and asked for the Minister's personal secretary. There was a wait of nearly five minutes, and then he spoke to the man who for six months had been his squadron commander in the rugged mountains to the northeast. He read the licence number of the taxi and the name of the *gringo* businessman who had gone in it. Then he mentioned a file with a particular number stored in the archives of the Department of State Security. The file was one of many dealing with corrupt commercial and industrial practices carried on by persons linked to the deposed dictator.

Late that night, three men in a jeep drove up to the door of a luxury hotel on the outskirts of the city and asked to see the fat white man with the identical leather suitcases who had come in a taxi that afternoon.

Miguel and The Mountain

Miguel sat on the edge of the crater at the top of the great volcano and knew that the sun was climbing up the sky in the east, even though he could not see it. He could not see the sun because he and all the top half of the mountain and the surrounding air were lost in a cloud that was made from water sucked out of the Pacific the day before and from the sulphurous steam that forever spiralled upwards and outwards from a small round hole deep down in the floor of the crater. He had watched the light creep into the cloud, changing the blackness of the long night into the ghostly steel-grey that enveloped him now in a clammy, swirling embrace, and he knew that he would die on the mountain before the sun rose again.

The irony of this death that was coming did not escape him. It was ironic because he was thirty-eight and in his prime, and because climbing mountains was not his profession, and because he had thought that his profession was a great deal more dangerous than climbing mountains. Miguel was a lorry driver. He had been a driver of lorries for exactly half his life — ever since he was nineteen.

His life had begun in these same islands where now it was ending. As a child growing up on one of the small outer islands he could see the mountain from the front doorway of the hut made of palm thatch and sticks that was his home. That picture was with him now and it warmed his mind and nearly made him forget the chill that had taken hold of his body and that would leave him only when the life force left him.

It was a blue picture. The sky was a light blue and the sea was a deep blue and the mountain was an in-between kind of dusty blue. There was a dabble of white in the picture too. Even on all those days when the rest of the sky was faultlessly blue, a small fluffy white cloud crowned the crater. Sometimes it was a candy-floss cloud that seemed to sprout from the bald head of the mountain. Other times it was a ring of white cotton encircling the cone of the crater. Still others, it was a blob of cream that had fallen on top of the mountain and run down to smear the sides.

He could never remenber a time when he had not wanted to climb the mountain. To climb it would have been a great and a wonderful and a grown-up thing to do. Groups of grown-ups came from the mainland and from other countries and once even from another continent to climb it. The islanders busied themselves with their primitive agriculture and ignored the mountain, except when the cloud grew denser and a faint smell of ash came on the wind and a noise like the low growling of a leopard reached them intermittently.

Then they remarked to each other that the volcano was stirring and their voices were tinged with concern and the older ones among them remembered that their fathers had seen the mountain's anger destroy two villages on its lower slopes and force the evacuation of all the inner islands for ten weeks because of the black ash that first filled the air and then settled, trying to smother everything that lived or grew or that men had built.

The mountain had its moods, the people said. It was best left alone. But Miguel had continued to dream. To dream about climbing the mountain was a great and a wonderful and a grown-up dream to have.

At one time it seemed that the dream would come true while he was still a teenager. All healthy young male Parivians were expected to do six months military service, and at seventeen Miguel was in khaki camouflage gear on the island of the big volcano. He was lean and restless then, with muscles that rippled all over his brown body when he moved. Even the heavy manual work building roads and a school and the forced marches in the jungle and the stolen nights spent courting the island girls did not use up all his energy.

But circumstances had prevented him from climbing the mountain. Training was confined to the lower slopes where vegetation grew. Parivia was a country of forests, and no guerrilla army or invading force would ever have to be confronted on the bare upper sides of a volcano. On the island they were driven too hard and kept too busy to have much time left over for conquering the mountain, and on leave periods Miguel always took the oily old cargo boat that chugged between the islands and went home to help his father with the crops.

It was during that half-year on the island of the volcano that his interest in the mountain became a kind of obsession. Every day he looked up beyond the vegetation to where the cone of the great mountain tapered away into the sky. A splash of white rock showed around the mouth of the crater. Below this for two thousand feet nothing grew and the mountain wore the red-brown colour of its vomited insides. Lower down, the *monte* took over and clothed the monster in green.

When he left the island for the last time he stood for a long while on the deck of the little boat and looked at the mountain. That day it seemed more majestic and unconquerable and alluring than ever before. Miguel cursed the opportunities he had let slip, and swore himself an oath that one day he would come back and win this battle that his mind fought always with the mountain.

The next year his father died and the family sold what they had and moved to the capital on the mainland. In the army Miguel had learned to drive. In the capital he drove an old wreck of a truck moving earth on a highway construction project. Afterwards he drove a better truck carrying materials from builders' yards in the city to sites scattered aroung the surrounding countryside. There were three brothers and four sisters and a mother who had become an old woman, and the brothers were not old enough to work except at shining shoes and selling newspapers. And Miguel wanted badly to get married.

He began to drive the big lorries: the kind that in the United States are called big rigs and in Parivia *furgónes*, to distinguish them from the smaller *camiónes*. At first he was a kind of irregular relief driver; when a regular driver was sick or suffering a loss of nerve or recovering from a mishap, Miguel drove in his place until the man was able to resume. In this way he drove many lorries and learned all that was to be known about driving big lorries. At twenty-two he was married with one child and a small concrete house of his own and he had a permanent job driving a *furgón* for a big company that had many lorries and drivers and hauled all kinds of freight.

Miguel regarded that lorry as his own. He had a right to, because only he drove it and slept in it and had it serviced and was always with it. His lorry had eighteen wheels — the ten of the cab section and the eight of the trailer. The engine hood was higher than his head and the cab had a dozen illuminated dials and two gear sticks.

The cab was beautifully finished in red paint, and the painting of the company's name, address and telephone numbers in yellow on the doors looked like works of art. The glistening brass klaxons mounted on the roof of the cab reminded him of trumpets. Attached to the cab at the back was the cubicle where he slept in the nights when he pulled weary-eyed off the road during the long trips. Miguel was proud of his lorry.

He was proud of his profession too, and of all the vast and

evergrowing army of workers who, by making possible the transport of its goods and raw materials to and between the cities and towns and the remote villages, made possible the continuation and further development of the kind of society that is called Western consumer.

There were first of all the drivers: the men who daily risked life and limb and nerves to bring whatever had been made from wherever it had been made or stored to wherever it was needed or wanted. There were the mechanics, who alone could keep the monsters on the road, and the service station hands who filled the huge tanks — set one on either side of the cab below the doors — with diesel. There was the industrial army that built the engines and the cabs and the trailers and made the tyres. And before them, the men who mined and smelted and forged the metals, and those who provided the rubber for the tyres and the paint for the bodywork.

Miguel was a careful driver. When the decade of the 1980s began he had been a driver almost half his life, without ever a major accident to report. He still worked for the same company, and the lorry he drove now was new, and his third since joining the company. The tyres alone were worth as much as the small family saloon his wife drove to get her to and from the suburban primary school where she was teacher.

Miguel drove often between the capital and the other growing industrial cities scattered around the great central mountainous plateau that is called the *altiplano*. He liked these shorter trips of fifty or a hundred or two hundred miles because they meant that on several nights each week he could be home in the little concrete house with his wife and four children and the dog and the colour T.V.

The long trips he liked less, though he would always like to drive, in the way that men like doing what they are good at. These trips could be of eight hundred or a thousand or even fifteen hundred miles each way, and took him to some of the most remote parts of the country. Often he went more than a week without seeing his family, and when he saw them it might be for only one or two days.

These journeys took him past the cold high cities of the *altiplano* and through its towns and villages, then on up north through the high desert country of hot days and cold nights and bare stone mountains and flat valleys full of dust and cactus plants and tufts of yellowed grass. Sometimes he drove all day on a thin strip of black asphalt that went always straight to the horizon, like a ribbon rolled out infinitely across the tawny parchment of the desert. On occasion he had to go down six or seven or maybe eight thousand feet to the cities of the coast where people made their living from tourism and fishing and trading and food processing. Then he drove using the engine as a brake, and stopping often with the wheels a yard from the edge of a precipice to make sure that the load in the trailer had not begun to shift.

On these long trips he would get up with the sun. He would rub his fingers through the thick black tangle of his hair and rub feeling into hands held between his knees and let the motor idle a few minutes — that powerful, throbbing engine that never failed to start as soon as he turned the ignition key. Then he would drive for two hours before he stopped for breakfast at some dusty little restaurant selling food that was less than he could eat and worse than he deserved and dearer than he should have had to pay, but whose faults were due to remoteness and therefore at least partly excusable.

In the early afternoon he would eat again, but not before attending to his lorry first, as a good cowboy would first see to the needs of his mount. With diesel tanks brimming, water level checked and tyres tapped to see if pressure was holding, he would treat himself to a scanty plate of meat and vegetables warmed and recently out of the restaurant's can, and three or four of the tasteless thin maize cakes called *tortillas*. All this he would wash down with two bottles of Coca Cola.

Late in the evening, with the sun low and its heat gone, he would stop to eat for the third time. When his meal was finished he would climb back up into the cab using the step cut into the petrol tank and the other on top of the tank, and he would drive until three or four hours after dark, stopping once or twice for a few minutes to rest eyes and renew concentration. When he felt satisfied with the distance he had covered he would turn off the asphalt at another restaurant, urge the lorry, lurching on the hard suspension, over the stony ground, and cut the engine.

After getting out briefly to urinate and stretch his legs, he would climb over the cab seat into the cubicle behind, roll himself fully clothed in the grey woollen blankets, and begin lightly to snore.

Miguel never stopped for a hitch-hiker. Reasons of time and speed and road safety ruled out non-essential stopping. But he carried many hitch-hikers from the restaurants and service stations and, less often, from some stopping place where he had pulled in to rest momentarily or to check the load. Bus and train travel in Parivia were among the world's cheapest because labour costs were low and the country had its own petroleum deposits and diesel was almost free, and so very few

Parivians ever hitched rides. For this reason, most of those that Miguel carried were young North Americans or Europeans in search of new experiences, and therefore a little more adventurous than the type of tourist who goes always in bus and train.

Those who travelled with Miguel always had their expectations fully rewarded. Miguel knew this, and for him it was one more among the many satisfying aspects of his job. Just to watch him drive fascinated them: the constant shifting of gears and the changes in engine tone; the effort needed in turning the steering wheel; the array of dials and switches; the cool, unhurried ease he brought to his job even at the most difficult times.

He knew too that part of the thrill for the passenger was the sense of danger that was always present. He sensed their unease whenever a little roughness came into the surface of the road, causing the fully-laden lorry driven in a high gear to act very much as a stubborn mule does. The lurching and bucking that resulted was the same in all the lorries — even the newest and most futuristically-equipped of them, but in travellers it usually inspired a sense of the nearness of possible disaster.

On steep descents, the sounds of the sophisticated braking systems soothed frayed travellers' nerves, and the precipices worried them only by day, in places where the road passed over unprotected bridges that crossed dizzying ravines, or where it had been cut from the solid rock of a mountainside.

Miguel well knew that the greatest danger came from none of these things, but from the long, straight, monotonous, narrow stretches of smoothly-surfaced fast road that often lasted for scores of miles. In the United States, these straight stretches caused few problems because oncoming traffic was always ten or even fifteen yards away on the other side of the median. But the Parivian Government could not afford to build highways with two wide lanes in each direction and the big trucks passed each other with a foot to spare on either side of the broken white line.

In a day's driving Miguel met upwards of three hundred lorries much like his own, and each one of those three hundred met the same number. On the straights there was never any room for error. On the curves it sometimes seemed that the gap of feet was being cut to inches as another truck approached. Then Miguel would move the wheel and to a passenger it would almost seem that the lorry danced a little sideways so that the gap remained a gap of feet and did not become a gap of inches.

Of all the uncounted millions of truck meetings that happened every year, only a handful of isolated cases ever ended in disaster. When the accidents happened, they were big. Drivers died. Trucks, and sometimes half a village, were destroyed. Sometimes the disaster happened because a front tyre blew out on a fast stretch or a braking system failed on a curve. More often, it happened because concentration was, for a second, lost.

In the rich countries there were stringent laws that told truck drivers the number of hours they were allowed to drive per day and per week. The authorities made a pretence of enforcing those laws. But the authorities and the drivers themselves and the people who owned the trucks knew that in practice there was no way of enforcing the time laws. In developing countries like Parivia, not even the pretence existed, and the truckers drove as far as their minds and bodies permitted and as fast as their lorries and their nerves allowed. They drove all day, and when night came they drove on and yawned and blinked red eyes and rolled their windows down and used their Citizens Band radios to talk with other drivers so that they could keep each other awake. And sometimes for a few seconds a driver slept, and if these few seconds came at a very bad time, the driver never woke up.

* * *

Miguel thought about all these things, and then he shivered and looked again into the greyness of the cloud that would not lift, and he began to think about how it was that he had come to be on the mountain.

For many months he had worked hard so that he had a lot of leave time due. Then he had taken three weeks and his wife and his four children and his dog and gone back to the islands for the first time in nearly twenty years. They stayed with the younger brother of his dead mother, on the island where he had been born. After four days in which he looked often at the mountain and four nights in which he thought often about it, Miguel had put some extra clothes and a pair of new sports shoes and a light sleeping bag in a worn rucksack, and taken the powerful modern hovercraft that now transported tourists from the outer islands to the island of the volcano.

In a small village in the shadow of the mountain, he bought some bread and cheese and a two-litre plastic container to carry water. He found a cheap lodging house and asked the woman who owned it to wake him before dawn, but only if there was no wind and the sky was clear enough to count the stars. In the morning there was cloud, and Miguel slept on. When evening came the clouds were lower. A mist hid the mountain. On the next afternoon the mist lifted and the grey skies cleared. On the third morning the landlady woke him just before dawn.

He pulled his clothes on and went outside. The noise of the *cicadas* and the winking of fireflies were the only signs of life besides his own. A full moon shone on the mountain and on the empty street. He stood to look for several minutes at the volcano. Then he went back in. He sat on the bed to tie his boots, went outside to the tap to splash water on his face, and came in again to get the plastic container. He filled it from the tap and hung it on his right shoulder by a cord tied to the handle. He slung the knapsack over his left shoulder.

Miguel waited to hear the weather forecast. The islands were expected to have dry weather. Winds would be light and variable. There would be some scattered cloud. Conditions would not be perfect that day either. But they were good enough for climbing the mountain. He had grown tired of waiting. His wait had not been a thing of days, but of decades.

His new North American sports shoes crunched on the black sand of the street. A dog barked. Behind him, at the other end of the village, a cock crowed. With the village behind him he followed the road that circled the island at the base of the volcano. He walked quickly because when the stars came out again he needed to be far down the mountain, below the high, dangerous places where there was only rock and sand and small, loose stones. With the food and the sleeping bag he carried in his knapsack, he could easily spend a night at the edge of the crater, but he knew that it would be better to keep going. If you slept in the cold places your body grew cold and a stiffness crept into the joints, and in the morning to go down would be hell.

Far away in the east, dawn poked with a ghostly grey finger at the bottom of the sky, but several hours would pass before he saw the sun. He would climb from the west, and so for a long time the mountain would hide the sun from him. He would go up the west side because that was the easiest way, and before the darkness came he would be halfway down the eastern side, and on the track that would take him to the village called Benque Viejo.

Only one star remained when he saw on his left the track that twisted its way through the dense foliage of the lower slopes and that had once led to the mining town of San Juan del Río. San Juan had been destroyed by the great eruption of January 1904, and no one except soldiers had ever lived there after that.

The trail was narrow and rutted and overhung with the rank green curtain of the forest. Consciously, Miguel slowed his pace as the ascent began. He felt cool and fresh and vigorous, but he needed to save his energy for the steepest part of the mountain where nothing grew, and where he would be in the early afternoon when the heat was greatest. For many years he had not felt such happiness. In three hours, or at most three and a quarter, he would reach the army camp. Some of those he had known might still be there, officers or instructors now. But there would not be much time for renewing old friendships: the mountain was waiting, and it had waited too long already.

The sky was blue and a warmth crept into the air. The cacophony of the forest was music in his ears. He walked in the jeep tracks, and his nostrils were full of the fresh green smell of the tropical morning. Yes; the mountain was waiting for him, as it had been waiting ever since he had been born. Today the waiting would end. Today was going to be his day.

The camp was built on the site where San Juan had stood eighty years before. Nothing remained of the town except for the site itself, which was a surprisingly level grassy platform at about twenty-two hundred feet. Irregular grass-covered mounds marked the places where the larger stone buildings had stood, but nothing was left of the thatch-and-timber huts where miners once lived with their families. The mines themselves had been sealed for ever with lava.

Miguel could see at once that the camp had changed. It now had a permanent look. Rows of long concrete buildings with roofs of corrugated iron painted jungle-green had replaced the make-shift bamboo structures of two decades earlier. Two dark-green helicopters sat on the grass near the edge of the clearing. The national flag flew high on a solitary steel flagpole set in concrete in the centre of the camp. At the entrance was a sentry-box with big glass windows, and a wooden barrier with a stop sign.

He spoke to the man on guard and was surprised to learn that he was from the capital on the mainland. They talked about the capital and about the changes that had come to the islands. Miguel found out that nearly all the men now in the camp were from the mainland, and none of his names or descriptions of old island comrades meant anything to the sentry.

He told the guard about his intention to climb the volcano, and about how it was a longstanding ambition with him. He bade the man goodbye and began to cross the clearing, intending to top up his water bottle and follow the course of the stream that flowed through the clearing, because there was still no road of any kind above the camp.

The sentry called him back to ask for his papers, and for the first time Miguel remembered that all his documents remained for safe keeping with his wife on the small outer island.

"Then you cannot pass this way", the guard said and his voice had lost its friendliness. Miguel offered to go around the camp, but the man said that this was not possible either; without papers, nobody was allowed in the area. He could stay in the camp that night. The next morning a jeep was due to go down to the village, and he would have to go with it.

Miguel was angry, but his anger did not show.

"I will speak with the commander of the camp", he said.

"Then you must wait," said the guard. Miguel sat on the ground beside the sentry box and watched the activities of the soldiers in their green and brown and khaki jungle camouflage uniforms, and he did not recognise a single one.

After more than two hours had passed, the sentry said that Captain Hernandez would see him now, and told him where to go. Miguel went to the small, square administration block fully determined to tell Captain Hernandez what he thought about him, his men and his camp. Then he forgot the speech that he had hotly assembled in his head. Captain Hernandez was none other than Miguel "El Toro" Hernandez, who twenty-one years before had been the only other Miguel in their platoon, and who had earned his nickname of "the bull" because of his squat, powerful appearance, his readiness to fight at the drop of a hat, and his often desperate quest for a girl — any girl — from among the island's population.

It was too late to continue the climb, and anyway there were a hundred new tales to be told and a thousand shared experiences to be laughed about. There was a guided tour of the camp, and even a short flight in one of the two ex-U.S. Army helicopters on its regular evening patrol.

At dawn the next morning Miguel climbed beside the river that had given the old town of San Juan del Río a part of its name. His stomach was heavy and he took only his water bottle and a little cheese and bread. The knapsack with the sleeping bag he left in the care of The

64

Bull Hernandez, who in two days, would meet him for a weekend of drinking and reminiscing in the village of Benque Viejo at the eastern foot of the mountain.

Miguel climbed slowly. He climbed slowly because his stomach was full of food and of the captain's wine, and because his head was full of the past. At the places where vegetation grew too dense, he climbed down into the river bed and clambered over the rounded rocks bordering the stream that ran low in its bed. Then he climbed out again and followed the bank as far as he could. But many times he had to go down into the gully.

By nine the river was behind him. Far below, the camp was lost in the matted green of the mountain. Above him towered the great barren cone of the volcano, its arid, lunar sides scarred by the gashes where water thundered for a few violent hours after rain. Miguel sat on a slab of honeycombed black rock to rest. Sweat soaked the hollow of his back and made big, damp circles in the armpits of his cotton shirt. He lifted his cap and adjusted the woollen jumper, tied by its sleeves around his neck, so that he could wipe the sweat from his forehead.

The top of the crater was lost in its white sulphury cloud, but this did not worry him, for he had expected it. Yet, the size of the cloud surprised him, until he realised that the reason was obvious; the wind had shifted so that, instead of ringing the top of the volcano, the cloud now lay entirely on the western side, hanging low along the mountainside directly above him. If he wanted to breathe fresh air until he reached the edge of the crater, he could not go up the west side, as had been his original intention. He drank a long draught from the plastic water bottle and resumed the ascent, now in a northwesterly direction.

This meant that soon he was no longer in the shadow of the mountain. He went more slowly now, sometimes walking in a painful, stooping position, sometimes almost crawling on all fours as the gradient increased and scree threatened to send him skidding hundreds of feet down the mountainside. A merciless sun beat down through the cotton shirt on his back and through the woollen jumper meant to protect his shoulders and upper back. Sweat drenched the hair under his cap and ran into his eyes and dripped steadily from the end of his nose and chin, and the water came hot from the idiot plastic bottle. And still the cloud hid the top of the mountain.

The sun climbs quickly in the tropics, then for many pitiless hours appears to stand still at the zenith, before sliding quickly down towards the western horizon. Miguel had known all of this since he was a child, and so when the sun seemed to stop directly above him, he was not afraid. He was climbing now on the more difficult eastern side, and yet the cloud hid the crater, and he knew that this cloud was big and covered the entire summit. He knew, too, that the cloud had not been shaped by wind, but rather by the absence of wind, and a small uneasiness came into his mind.

By mid afternoon his head ached and sourness cramped his stomach. To go up on the eastern side was torturously slow and it was dangerous, but now at least he was safe from the sun. He was glad that he was wearing sports shoes and not conventional climbing boots. The shoes were lighter and gave great flexibility to the feet, helping him to get toeholds in crevices where the ascent was steepest.

Once only, he looked down. He saw the long, grey-brown, tilted desert beneath him and wondered how he had climbed it. Somewhere below him, a grey, wispy cloud hung motionless over the forested slopes. A desperate longing seized him and he wanted to go back down, to get off the cursed, evil mountain before night came and while strength was still in his body and hope still in his soul.

But even then he knew he would go on. With half his mind he knew that he had to climb this mountain now. His wife and his children had heard him speak often of the mountain. They all knew how badly he wanted to climb it. He could not face them with failure in his eyes. Above all, he could not face himself if he failed, for he would never come back to the mountain. Soon he would be in middle age. Even now, he was less a man than he had thought himself, and that was hard to bear. Driving lorries could make you a man. But driving lorries could not make you a climber of mountains.

There was another reason too why he would go on. This other reason had the other half of his mind, though he did not yet admit it to himself. It was fear. He was afraid to go back down where he had come up. He climbed. He smelled the sulphur. It was slight at first: another small unpleasantness to add to the catalogue of bodily discomforts and mental anxieties.

Miguel scrambled higher, and the cloud closed around him. Part of the cloud was water vapour that had risen from the ocean eight thousand feet below. Such cloud made things look cold and grey and strange and it brought the distance a man could see down to a few yards, but Miguel thought that with a cloud such as that a man could live. The rest of the cloud too was vapour, but this vapour was rising

66

from the bowels of the mountain and it was full of the minerals and gases of the earth. It made him cough and gave him a half-choking feeling. It hung in his nostrils, in his throat, and even, it seemed, in his stomach. He no longer knew how far he had to go, but he climbed on. He no longer cared about pride and ambition and about his need to beat the mountain. Fear drove him higher. It was almost as if some kind of sanctuary awaited him at the edge of the crater; almost as if he would be safe there from the terrors that surrounded him.

Miguel reached the edge of the crater. He lay on his stomach and looked down into it, but he could see nothing except the great, billowing clouds of steam spiralling upwards and outwards, filling the vastness of the crater; seeming even to fill the vastness of the sky above the crater.

He had read about the mountain and he knew that the crater was 840 feet deep, with vertical walls of black and red-brown solidified lava. The floor of the crater, he had read, was of black lava and was littered with loose rocks. In the centre of the crater floor was a hole less than one hundred feet across, and 330 feet deep, and from this crater came the swirling clouds of sulphurous vapour. The small crater was called The Mouth of Hell. On days when conditions were right and there was not too much steam, the molten red lava could be seen, even from certain positions twelve hundred feet above on the edge of the main crater.

The sweat of the climb dried on him as he lay there and a shiver gripped his body. Lifting himself into a sitting position he struggled into the jumper, but the cold remained. The only sound was the faint hiss of steam in the crater. He might have been on another planet — an alien, desert world with a noxious atmosphere and no life, of man or animal or plant, except his own.

If you climbed El Vulcan Del Diablo, the books had said, you would reach a height of 9,213 feet above the Pacific Ocean. It had been well named. It was indeed The Devil's Volcano. The people of the islands said that no man should climb alone on The Devil's Mountain lest the Devil punish him. Miguel had not listened, and now he was being punished. But he knew that this punishment was not of Satan's making. It was the revenge of the mountain. Long before reaching the top he had begun to pay, and the mountain's price was high, and he knew it would be higher.

He finished the water and for a moment it banished the taste of sulphur from his mouth. He replaced the cap on the plastic bottle and dropped it into the crater. There was no water within three thousand feet; there would be none without several dangerous hours of climbing. Miguel thought about the river more than three thousand feet below him, and of the ocean more than nine thousand feet below, and he thought of the water that was in the air all around him. He tried to remember the Rhyme of the Ancient Mariner that was in the old book of poems he kept in the lorry. The book was a collection of the world's most famous poems. He remembered only a few scattered lines.

It was time to go down. His watch said 4.10. One and a half hours of daylight remained. Then his bowels opened and the rancid, stinking smell in his clothing overwhelmed the smell of the sulphur. He stood feebly, using his hands, and liquid excrement ran down his legs and dripped from the ends of his trousers onto his ash-blackened shoes.

Trembling, he sat down. He untied the shoes and took them off. Slowly, he removed his clothes. He dropped the yellowed, soaking briefs over the crater's edge. Then he stood again, and with the sweat-sodden cotton shirt wiped his buttocks and legs dry. He used it too to wipe the seat and crotch of the trousers inside. Then he threw the shirt away, but he did not throw it into the crater. He pulled the wet, fouled trousers on, and was pulling the jumper over his head when his bowels opened again.

This time he did not take his trousers off. He sat on the ground and put his feet in his shoes and did the laces, and then he cried. He tried to get up, but no power was in his legs. With a cold sweat on his forehead, he lay with his back against a lump of lava and waited and waited to see if strength would return.

From below came the sound of a helicopter. It was the five o'clock evening patrol. The noise increased momentarily and brought a wild, unreasoning hope, but the hope died along with the whirr of the rotor blades. He was shaking. A numbing coldness had invaded his body and an invisible, chilling terror had seeped in and filled the vacant corners of his mind. He knew that he could not stand and so he lay in the wetness of his shit, and shivered and waited for the darkness.

In the morning he wondered how he had lived through the night. It had been a night that lasted for all eternity. He had spent it sitting, with his legs straight and his hands tucked under his arms, swaying slowly from side to side and moving his toes. Probably his mind had kept him alive. At times he had imagined that he might yet get off the mountain when the new day came. Maybe the cloud would lift. He might regain proper use of his legs. The bouts of dysentry might stop, and strength return to his body. He might not fall if he attempted the descent. The Bull Hernandez might even send a helicopter to look for him.

A hundred times in the long night he thought these thoughts, and a hundred times his senses told him that he was a fool to think them. His hands touched the course, sandy ash and the hard rock of the mountain top. His nose was full of the smell of sulphury gases, and his mouth was full of the taste of them. His ears heard only the hiss of the steam, and his eyes saw nothing but darkness.

*   *   *

The sun continued its climb up the sky, but a sour wind ruffled the calm of the Pacific and a great bank of grey-black cloud hid the top half of the mountain. Beneath the cloud a dull green helicopter flew low over the forest. Miguel did not hear the helicopter. He was seeing his picture.

It was a blue picture. The sky was a light blue and the sea was a deep blue and the mountain was an in-between kind of dusty blue.